I0544069

Actions Have Consequences

All Things are Only for God

By Gerald C. Anderson, Sr.

Lyfe Publishing

Publishers Since 2012

Published by Lyfe Publishing LLC

Lyfe Publishing, 10800 Nautica Place, White Plains MD 20695

ACTIONS HAVE CONSEQUENCES

Library of Congress Cataloging in Publications Data

Gerald C. Anderson, Sr.

Actions Have Consequences / Gerald C. Anderson, Sr.

ISBN: 978-1-957333-14-4

(Fictitious Character)-Fiction

Washington DC

Actions Have Consequences–Fiction

Printed in the United States of America

1 2 3 4 5 6 7 8 9 10

Book design by Olivia Pro Designs and Lyfe Designs

Editor

Beryl Anthony Brackett

Chief Editor

BAB Productions, LLC

18103 Merino Drive

Accokeek, Maryland 20607

ACKNOWLEDGEMENT

Thank you for your support with "Actions Have Consequences"

Beryl Anthony Brackett

Danny Sells

Danyelle Speaks

Avis Dillard-Bullock

Also, By Gerald C. Anderson, Sr.

We Come in Peace

27 Hours

Standing Firm

Secrets

The Last Song

The Lawyer

Saved

The Room

Are You Innocent?

The Compendium Series

Weight Loss

Warlord

The Last Honorable Man

The Dream

The Death Knights

Twins

The Ride Along

Creative Inspirations

Fatal Misperceptions

Love & Lust

Where is Erica Cousins (Kindle Vella)

Prologue

It was a warm summer morning when Derek James woke from his sleep. He looked over and watched his wife sleeping normally. He admired her beauty and counted himself the luckiest man in the world.

The year before, doctors told Derek he could not have a child, but God proved them wrong and now he was on the verge of being a father. It would be the proudest moment of his life. He was nervous. Derek took being a father as a serious life choice, and he was concerned, hoping that he would make all the right choices. He stopped thinking about that. He would be a great father and he knew it.

Derek went downstairs to his makeshift laboratory. He was enamored with time travel and the possibilities of making it happen.

He sat at his computer and performed calculations he started the night before. It was not long before he heard his name shouted in the loudest, scariest tone he could imagine.

Derek jumped up and ran upstairs to see what was going on with his wife. "Honey, what's wrong?"

"My water broke!"

Her words caught Derek by surprise. He imagined he would know what to do in this situation, but now it was time and he hesitated. She shouted again, "Derek, my water broke!"

"Yes, yes… let's go. Where's your bag?"

"By the door."

"Okay, okay… let's do this." The couple jumped in their Honda CR-V and headed to the hospital. Derek tried to conceal his nervousness, but the traffic was getting to him. It was early morning, and the road was filled with drivers making their way to work.

Derek said, "Forget this. I'm getting us there!"

"Derek, you're on the shoulder. You're going to kill us."

"No, I'm not. Just relax, I'll get us there." She laughed. "Why are you laughing, baby?"

"You're the nervous one. You need to relax."

Derek chuckled. He was the nervous one. He thought about this day for a while and now it was here. His son was going to be born. He smiled at the thought of creating a little scientist. Someone to follow in his footsteps.

Derek maneuvered his way through traffic and onto Andrews Air Force Base. They rushed into the hospital and the nurse checked them in. It was not long before Derek realized that his erratic driving was unnecessary. It would be ten hours before Derek James Jr. would be born.

Ten hours later, Derek officially became a father. He held little Derek in his arms, admiring the work he and Monica James created. "He's so handsome, I can't wait to give him his first science kit." Everyone laughed.

Five Years Later

Derek could not believe his son was now five years old. The years were flying by and the love for his son grew to proportions no one could imagine. He exposed him to science and continued to pray he would follow in his footsteps.

It was Wednesday and Derek's normal day to take his son to the park while Monica made dinner. This was his alone time with the boy they nicknamed DJ. "DJ, are you ready?"

"Almost dad," he shouted from his upstairs bedroom where Monica was getting him dressed.

Today Derek and DJ would explore solar heat by making a solar heat chimney. He checked his gear to make sure he had everything. *"Let's see, I got the empty pop cans, masking tape, matte black spray paint, tin snips, but where's my infrared digital thermometer?"*

Derek searched his laboratory until he found the thermometer. DJ and Monica were still upstairs. *"They are so slow."* "Let's go DJ." Finally, I could hear the pitter patter of his tiny feet. DJ met him at the door and Monica smiled at the two of them. "Well, it's about time, buddy."

DJ laughed, "Da-ddy."

"Let's go." Derek and DJ kissed Monica goodbye. They hurried out the door, but Derek was surprised when he saw a suspicious looking man standing near their car. The man looked at Derek and DJ. Derek said, "Are you looking for someone?"

The man replied, "Yeah, you, my man."

"We don't want any trouble."

"Good. Give me the keys to your car."

Derek looked at his son, "It's okay, buddy." Derek felt his son ease behind him. "Okay, take the keys. Just leave us alone."

The man caught the keys after Derek tossed them to him. "You think you're better than me, don't you?"

"No, I don't. Just take the car, man."

"Don't tell me what to do. You some kind of teacher or something?"

"No, I'm a scientist."

"Oh yeah, you think you better than me."

"I don't. Just leave me and my son alone."

The man turned toward the car but quickly turned back. He pointed the gun at Derek, and Derek pushed his son behind him.

The shots rang out throughout the neighborhood. Derek fell to the ground, ensuring he covered his son. The last thing he heard was the man telling DJ, "Now, you're like me."

Chapter 1

"To everything there is a season and a time to every purpose under the Heaven." Ecclesiastes 3:1.

25 Years Later

DJ struggled in his sleep. The dream was stirring in his mind. He viewed Washington, DC, from the top of a building. There was no hustle or bustle as it always is in the city. Today, no one was left alive.

Bodies were across the streets. Cars were parked with windows bashed out, apparently stolen days before the thief died of the deadly virus.

The dream moved him down to the streets. The stench was real to him. Some bodies were there for weeks, maybe months, while others only hours or days.

He felt a hand touch him on the shoulder. DJ turned and jumped at the sight of a woman whose face was etched with sores, puss oozing out of some of them. She had the virus and now she touched him.

He jumped at another touch. DJ's eyes popped open, and he stared at his lovely wife, Tameka. She giggled at him, knowing he must have been dreaming. He asked, "What's so funny?"

"Dude, you were screaming. I'll meet you downstairs."

He continued to wake from his dream. *"That seemed so real. All those bodies, people dead or dying from a virus. Instead of time travel, I should try to figure out how to prevent something like that from happening."*

DJ washed up and got dressed. He made his way downstairs. He looked at his beautiful wife, Tameka, with admiration. In his mind, there was no one else like her. She stood by him when no one else would. His ideas about time travel made him into the laughingstock of the science community, but he vowed not to give up on his father's work. No one understood his deep feelings for finishing the work his father started then using that work to travel back to save him. He noticed Tameka looking at him over her coffee, smiling. He asked, "What?"

She answered, "You look so deep in thought. What are you thinking about?"

He replied, "The usual."

Tameka sat down at the kitchen table with him, and said, "You had another dream, didn't you?" He nodded. "What was this one about?"

DJ continued to hesitate. He did not want to get into a discussion with her. Yes, she supported him, but he felt deep inside she thought it was a waste of time as well. "Honey let's not get into this today. It's a beautiful morning. Let's talk about something else."

"It's overcast, so not beautiful. Tell me about the dream."

He could not wear her down. She was going to press him until he told her about the dream. "Okay baby, I see we're on a mission this morning."

"It's because I love you." She winked her eyes sealing the deal even more.

"It was a weird dream. I was standing on top of a building in DC. I couldn't tell which one, but there was no movement on the streets. Everything was dirty and smelled awful. It was death everywhere."

Tameka's eyes widen, "Wow, let's hope that doesn't happen."

DJ nodded his head, "Yeah, that's for sure."

Tameka responded, "I think this is because you haven't told the one story you need to tell."

"Here we go."

"Come on, baby. I'm your wife and you've never told me."

"I have."

"Not the entire story." DJ did not respond. He hoped something would come up and he would not have to answer. The plan did not work. Tameka continued to press. "Honey, you need to get this off your chest once and for all. You have never completely talked this through with anyone, including me. After all, you were only five when it happened, right?"

He responded, "Almost six."

She continued, "Funny, Mr. James, now tell it to me. I'm not going anywhere until you talk."

He looked down, pondering his next words. He loved her and he needed her in his life. If anyone should hear the story from his own words, it should be Tameka, but he was not sure he could do it. DJ said, "I don't know if I can."

Tameka sternly said, "Derek James Junior, don't make me..."

He knew she was getting angry when she called him 'Derek James Junior. He decided it was time to tell her his story about that dreadful day, 25 years ago. "Okay", he started, "As you know it was 25 years ago in the summer. Me and my parents were in the house.

We still lived in the townhouse where I first met you. We hadn't moved yet."

"This particular evening dad was taking me to the park. He enjoyed spending father and son alone time with me. Mom didn't know it, but he often told me he did. Anyway, mom helped me get dressed and put my shoes on. I hugged mom and ran to the door where dad was waiting. That's one thing I always remember about my dad. He always waited at the door for me and mom. That was his thing. Anyway, we went outside, and I was jumping up and down with excitement. Dad said as he usually did, *'Boy, what's wrong with you?'* I just laughed and gave my usual answer, 'Daddy!'"

"I never noticed the man approaching us from the left. I think my dad did. He kept looking that way and tried to hurry me along, but the man cut us off. He told daddy to give him the keys to our car. Daddy reached in his pocket and tossed the keys to him and told the man to take the car and don't shoot us. I remember daddy pleading, 'I have a son.'"

"That's when the man looked coldly at daddy and shot him twice in the chest. I remembered the sound of the gun being so loud that I wet my pants. I felt the life go out of my dad as his hand let go of my hand and he fell to the ground. He covered me, but my head was still out, and I could see the man. To this day, I see it in my mind; in slow motion."

"Daddy was lying on the ground, the blood slowly easing away from him, soaking his shirt and my clothes. I just laid there scared out of my life, glad my dad was covering me so the man couldn't shoot me. My pants were wet and bloody. I was too scared to even cry."

"After what seemed like hours, the man said to me, 'Now you're like me'. He jumped in our car and drove off. I cried and cried until my mom came out of the house. She fell to her knees, grabbed me, and both of us cried until the police came."

Tameka gasped and wiped the tears from her eyes. "I'm so sorry you experienced that." She stood and embraced her husband. DJ loved the feeling of her against him. After telling that story for the first time in 25 years, he needed her warm embrace.

Chapter 2

Tameka knew parts of the story of her husband's father's death, but she never heard her childhood friend and now husband tell it from his perspective.

She fought the tears as he told the story, knowing she needed to console him. Thoughts of the man she knew as Mr. Derek ran through her mind.

She remembered how Mr. Derek taught her to play the guitar. She was always scared to come to her lesson when she hadn't practiced but he never yelled at her. Secretly, she liked him for that. After his death, she became close to DJ. She was three years older, but that never bothered them. Her mother and her husband's mother became close as well. She liked Ms. James, and the two of them often spent time together.

Tameka continued to hold her husband. She said, "I know it's been hard for you, but I will always be here for you. Never forget that."

DJ responded, "I haven't, and I never will forget." She smiled as they both looked deeply into each other's eyes.

Tameka asked, "If you're successful with this time machine and you go back in time to save your father; won't that stop us from being together?"

DJ answered, "There's no way that would happen. I would love you and be with you no matter what timeline we're in."

She smiled. Inside, she felt the same way. She loved her husband and would continue to stand by him, no matter what. He was the laughingstock of the scientific community, but she knew it didn't bother him, so it didn't bother her either. He would continue his work and she would continue to stand by him.

Tameka said, "Well, Mr. James, I have to go to work and so do you. Make that time machine work, baby." She kissed him like the first time she ever kissed him. She wanted him to know how much she loved him. Tameka grabbed her keys and walked out the door, smiling as she knew he was watching her walk. She said seductively, "Stop looking at my behind."

Once outside, she released the floodgates, and the tears roared down her face. She sat in the driver's seat, trying to understand how something could happen to such a great man and his family. It changed them so much.

Tameka drove off to work. She could not stop thinking about the story her husband told her. She knew he embellished some details because he was only five when it happened. It was a horrible experience. *"I'm so glad he threw himself into science to follow in his father's footsteps. Time machine or not, he is a great scientist."*

She arrived at work and met her best friend Sade at the door. "Hey, Sade, how are you?"

"Good, girl. I wish I had gotten some sleep last night."

"What happened? You met someone?"

"Yeah. I met him in Petersburg for dinner."

Tameka popped her lips, "Petersburg? That's two hours away. Why couldn't he come to you?"

Sade sighed, "I volunteered to go there. We met online, and he's in Petersburg for a convention. He lives in Atlanta. Anyway, this clown had dinner with me then drove around Petersburg, showing me around. Finally, I reminded him I needed to get back on the road. He kept saying, just one more time. Then he said, you know you can always stay overnight."

"What? No, he didn't."

"Yes, he did. He was trying to keep me out late so I would be too tired to drive home. I told that clown to take me back to my car right then."

"I know that's right."

"So needless to say, I'm so exhausted right now."

"Ah, I'll get us some coffee."

"That would be awesome, Tameka."

Tameka went to the coffee shop in the basement of their building. They served the best coffee, and she loved their breakfast sandwiches as well. She returned to her desk, which was next to Sade's desk. Tameka handed Sade the coffee and sandwich. "Here you go, my friend. This should make you feel better."

"Oh, I'm sure it will. How was your evening?"

Tameka sat down and booted up her computer, "Pretty much uneventful. Me and DJ had dinner. He made his famous jambalaya and then we watched the new Batman movie."

"How was it?"

"It sucked to me, but he loved it. We have drastically different taste in movies." Sade chuckled. "Hey, we make it work. Next time I get to choose the movie and it won't be a superhero one."

"Technically, Batman isn't a superhero. He doesn't have special powers." Tameka rolled her eyes at Sade. "Okay, enough about that." They both laughed.

Evan came to Tameka's desk. Tameka asked, "What can I do for you, Evan?"

"How about a date?" She rolled her eyes at him. "Okay, maybe not, but can I buy you another coffee?"

"Evan, we've had this conversation too many times. I am not interested in cheating on my husband. Can you leave it alone? You're bordering on harassment."

Sade said, "Bordering? Child, he's way past that border."

Evan said, "I see. I won't bother you again." He walked away.

Sade continued, "In another life, you two could have been an item."

"In another life, I'd still be with Derek James Jr."

Chapter 3

After Tameka left, DJ pondered his problems. He really missed his dad, and he knew his mom missed him as well. She never remarried after his father's death. Sometimes he wondered if it was because of him and his love for his father. He continued to hold on to the hope of one day building this time machine and going back to save his father.

The solution to his wormhole theory of time travel continued to elude him. It seemed to be right in his reach, but still 10,000 miles away. Ironically, all he needed was more time. He was scheduled to meet up with his friend and assistant, Jeff Burton, in a few minutes. He got himself together and hurried down to the basement.

DJ worked as a scientist at a premier laboratory in Maryland. Radford Technology was owned by the renowned scientist Anthony Radford. Anthony hired him because he knew DJ was special. He continued to support him even after DJ's theories about time travel came out and the community laughed and ridiculed him.

DJ decided not to go into work today. Instead, he worked in his basement with Jeff. Jeff was a scientist who graduated from the University of Maryland with the highest honors. He had the same passion as DJ in time travel. Together, they both believed they could make it work.

DJ tinkered with some equations in the basement when he heard a faint sound in the background. It was the doorbell. He didn't know how long it had been ringing, but he figured it was Jeff.

DJ ran up the stairs to the main level and answered the door. "I'm so sorry, man. I hope you weren't out there long," he explained. Jeff just shook his head and smiled. DJ knew Jeff was all too familiar with his habits. He knew DJ would engross himself into his work and sometimes he couldn't hear or see anyone or anything else.

Jeff said, "Man, I've been out here for 20 minutes, but I knew you were in here, so I just kept ringing that dang doorbell. I knew eventually you would hear it."

They both laughed. Jeff was right. DJ said, "Man, you know me."

Jeff responded, "Yeah, I do... any progress?"

DJ answered, "Nothing. I can't wrap my head around the calculations to keep the bridge stable or reintegrate matter once we get to the other side. If I get it stable, I can't seem to get pass the reintegration issue. Then there's the return trip back. This won't do any good if I can't come back home."

Jeff replied, "That is true, my friend. I've been doing some calculations and research on our Einstein-Rosen bridge. I think I may have the solution."

"Really," Derek replied, "What's your solution?"

"Here, check this out," Jeff handed him a notebook with his most current calculations. Derek looked at them twice and smiled.

He looked up and said with enthusiasm, "This might work." They both rush downstairs to the basement and entered the new equations into their computer. After 30 minutes, DJ stepped back from his computer. It was another failure. DJ did not know how many more of these he could handle, but inside he knew he had to press on. "It didn't work."

Jeff replied, "I was so sure it would work. What do we do now?"

"I don't know. I need a break."

"Okay, I'll continue to do some work and see what I can come up with."

"Thanks Jeff. We have to make this work." DJ rushed upstairs and to his car. He felt the stench of failure even if Jeff did not. Jeff was always more optimistic than he was. DJ rode to his favorite spot by the pond. The park was near his home, and he loved it. Beautiful trees and freshly cut grass surrounded the flowing pond water. The serenity of it all calmed his mind.

After an hour of thought, he returned to his lab, where Jeff continued to be hard at work. DJ said, "Man, you haven't moved an inch."

"We got to get this to work, brother."

"I understand my motivation, but what exactly is yours?"

Jeff looked up from his work, "Are you serious, man? If we discover a method to travel back in time, we would be on par with Einstein, Newton, Galilei, all the big boys. Our names will be alongside of them. That's motivation enough, don't you think?"

"I guess I never gave that much thought. All I want to do is finish my dad's work and go save him."

Jeff sighed, "Have you thought anymore about the ramifications of such an action? You don't know what could happen."

"I would have more time with my dad. That's the only ramification I care about."

Jeff continued, "But what about the world, man?"

"The world, Jeff? My dad was a scientist like me. I'm not having much impact on the world. Why would he? If we get this to work, I'm going to go back and save my dad."

"Okay, I just think you should give it some thought. Do I need to explain the butterfly effect to you?"

"Yeah, why don't you quote that to me again?"

"A property of chaotic systems by which slight changes in initial conditions can lead to a large-scale and unpredictable variation in the future state of the system. Saving your dad may be a small change to you, but it could have a large-scale effect."

"You know I was being rhetorical, right?"

"I know, but I wanted to quote it to you, anyway. Give you something to think about."

"Well, Jeff, we aren't close to solving our equations, so it's a moot point." DJ did not like the conversation. He understood the butterfly effect and how changing one seemingly small item can have a significant effect on the world, but he refused to believe saving his father mattered to anyone outside his family. It was something he would do no matter what the ramifications.

Both worked quietly through the rest of the morning while gaining no apparent ground on solving the mystery behind time travel. Jeff headed out to be with his wife while DJ prepared for Tameka's return from work.

Tonight, the couple would entertain Tameka's sister, Angela, and her husband, Chaquille. DJ had no great love for Chaquille. They were opposites, mostly. Chaquille played one year in the NFL before he blew out his knee and had to retire. Now he searched for a coaching position at any level.

Angela was vibrant and full of joy. She had her ways, but DJ liked her and since he did not have siblings, it was great to have Angela.

Tameka burst through the door. "You will not believe my day, honey." She kissed him on the lips and continued without giving DJ a chance to respond. "That bastard, Evan. Ugh, he gets on my nerves!"

"What did he do now?"

"The same stuff. All day he kept flirting with me. I asked him to stop, but he would just come back again. I'm going to file a complaint against him." Again, she continued before he could respond. "Sade said I should have filed two weeks ago, but I wanted to give the brother a chance. I didn't want him to go down, but I can't take it anymore."

DJ knew she was upset when he couldn't get a word in edge wise. He simply choose to listen to her vent about her day and occasionally smile or agree with whatever she said. He loved her and decided years ago that sometimes it was necessary to listen to your spouse vent than to inject your personal thoughts. Tameka often listened to him when he was upset. He admired this about their marriage.

When she was done, Tameka took a deep breath and smiled at DJ. "DJ, honey, thank you so much for listening to me rant and rave. I think you think I'm losing my mind, but sometimes it's good to get it off my chest." She hugged him and laid her head on his chest. "I love you, honey."

"I love you too, Tameka. Listening to you rant, is my pleasure. I know you sit and listen to mine when I go off about something in the scientific community. It's all good."

She released him and planted a kiss on his lips. "How about a little something before our guest arrive?"

DJ smiled, "Oh, early evening sex? I'm down." They both laughed and headed upstairs. Like most men, DJ lived for that time with his wife. He could not imagine him loving another woman. Each time they made love, it felt like the first time to him. Her immaculate ebony body was cut so finely it could be considered the world's best jewel stone. The time she spent in the gym paid off in her looks. He thought, *"I'm the luckiest man in the world. A gorgeous wife, with a tight body and a dedicated mind. What more could I ask for?"*

Tameka fell off of DJ, exhausted from their sexual experience. DJ loved her on top of him and he believed she loved it, too. He looked into her big brown eyes and fell in love again. She snuggled under his arm and the two fit together like they were never meant to be anywhere else. DJ said, "That was awesome as usual, baby. You're so talented."

"Oh, honey, you're the talented one, but we need to get up and get dressed for our company."

"Do we have to?"

Tameka hopped up, "Yes, get up and get dressed to entertain my sister and her husband. Come on, dude."

"Okay, but if Chaquille says one thing…"

Tameka pecked him on the lips, "No, honey, be nice. He's not in the best of moods these days."

"Yeah, blowing out your knee and ending a multi-million dollar career isn't easy to take, but don't make us all suffer because you're down."

"I know, but maybe you can put in a word for him at the high school he's applying at. They need a coach, and you gave a few speeches to the science department. They respect you."

DJ did not want to do it. Chaquille never considered DJ as an equal. He believed he was better than DJ because he was scheduled to make millions in the NFL. Now he was jobless and wanted DJ to put in a word for him. DJ knew he would never hear the end of it from Tameka. "Okay honey, I'll call the principal tomorrow."

"Thank you, baby."

DJ got dressed and ran downstairs. As usual, Tameka was taking a little longer. DJ broke out the wine glasses and a bottle of their best wine. He placed it in the bucket with some ice to let it chill before their guest arrived. DJ shouted upstairs, "Baby, are you dressed yet?"

She shouted back, "Almost."

DJ thought to himself, *"Almost means another hour. At least Angela is just as slow as Tameka. Definitely runs in the family."* DJ flicked the television on and got comfortable. There was an old science fiction movie on. He laughed at all the mistakes while he waited for everyone to arrive.

DJ fell asleep on the couch, waiting. The worst day of his life played out again in his dream. He was not sure if he made up the details or remembered them, but the murder of his father clearly rolled through his mind. The slow motion effect had to be added by the dream makers. He watched his father fall to the ground again and again until suddenly she woke him. "Dreaming again?" That smirky smile on her face made him laugh.

"Yeah." He eased up to regain his senses.

Tameka continued, "I guess you didn't hear the doorbell either." She pointed to her lips, "You got a little something right here." She laughed again.

"Oh, you got jokes now." He watched her open the door and greet her sister. Angela was a petite young woman who DJ admired. He felt Chaquille did not deserve such a good woman.

Angela rushed over to DJ and hugged him tight. She said in his ear, "Be nice, brother-in-law."

"Always little sister."

Angela continued, "We brought some wine for the evening." She looked at Chaquille and DJ, then continued, "Well, Tameka, how about we put this wine on ice?"

Tameka said, "Yeah, let's." Tameka patted DJ on the chest and walked into the kitchen with Angela.

DJ said, "So, what's up, Chaquille?"

"This job. Are you going to put in a word for me?"

"Straight to it." DJ popped his lips, "Dude, I'm concerned about your temper. If I put my name on the line for you and you blow up like you did against the refs in Miami, what's that going to do to me?"

"I'm not that guy anymore, DJ. Look, I blew out my knee and lost everything. I went from millions to barely making it. I need this job, if for no other reason but to feel like a man again." DJ considered his words. They were convincing, but he still hesitated. "DJ, how would you feel if your wife were the breadwinner in the family?"

DJ dropped his head and grinned, "Chaquille, my wife makes more money than I do. She has been for a few years now. It's no issue for the wife to make more than the husband. Don't worry, you will regain your manhood. Actually, you never lost it." Chaquille stood staring at him. He knew Chaquille was a man who believed he was supposed to make the money in the household. DJ said, "Look, I will talk to the principal about the position first thing in the morning, but I need to know for sure that will not blow up on me."

"You have my word as a man. I'm not the man I used to be when I played. That Miami incident was blown way out of proportion. The refs didn't take any action against Thomas, just me. I complain and I'm made out to be a menace."

DJ sighed, "You have to own up to it, man. If they ask you about it, you need to take responsibility."

Before Chaquille could answer, the ladies returned to the room. Tameka said, "I hope all is good here."

DJ didn't not want to answer. He felt bullied by Tameka, Angela and Chaquille to vouch for Chaquille when he did not want to. To keep the peace, he towed the line. "Everything is fine. Is the food ready?"

The doorbell rang. Tameka replied, "It is now." Everyone laughed, knowing Tameka ordered dinner instead of cooking it. She walked to the door and retrieved the food. She continued, "Let's eat."

DJ loved her, but she could not cook at all. He did not care, though. DJ said, "So, what did you order, honey?"

"I got the family meal from our favorite Italian restaurant. Everyone loves pasta. DJ, can you pray over the food?"

DJ looked at her. She knew he lacked confidence in certain areas of his life, and this was one of them. He feared speaking or praying in public. Angela said, "Dude, you're the man of the house. You can handle it."

He wanted to choke her, but he prayed, "Dear Heavenly Father, we thank you for bringing us together today; keeping us safe from all harm and danger. We thank you for our health and spirits. We pray that Chaquille nails down this head coaching position. Most of all, we pray for this food that is about to nourish our bodies. In your son Jesus' name, we pray... Amen."

Angela replied, "See, that was awesome, and thank you for that kind word for my husband. Right, Chaquille?"

"Sure, honey."

DJ frowned. *"The least he could do is appreciate it."*

Angela said what DJ thought, "You could show some appreciation, honey."

Chaquille frowned, "I appreciate you guys and your belief in God, but where was he when I blew out my knee and lost my career?"

Angela replied, "That's enough of that, Chaquille. Don't ruin this evening with my sister and her husband."

"You asked."

Tameka said, "Everyone blames God for their problems, but they lack service. You don't go to church or anything, yet God is supposed to do everything for you. How about you do something for Him?"

No one replied. She continued. "That's what I thought."

Everyone ate quietly until Tameka broke the silence. "Okay, everyone, how about we talk about something else?"

Angela answered, "Sounds good to me." She looked at DJ, "How's that science project going?"

DJ snickered, "You make it sound like a school project or something." Angela turned her head sideways slightly. DJ continued, "It's going. We still haven't had the breakthrough we need."

Tameka asked, "Time travel isn't easy to solve."

Angela replied, "I don't think anyone should play God with time. If you change something, then everyone's life could be affected."

"Saving my dad's life will only affect my life. Nothing major will change."

Chaquille responded, "I'm sure Dr. Frankenstein said the same thing when he created the monster."

DJ's frustration showed on his face. "Are you really comparing a 19th century science fiction movie to what I'm doing in real life?"

Chaquille answered, "My point is every time man tries to be God, it goes all wrong. Want a real life example? How about the atomic bomb? Oppenheimer regretted playing God by creating it. He said he became death."

DJ nodded his head, "Oppenheimer created a weapon of mass destruction. I'm creating a way for mankind to travel in the past. There is a significant difference."

Angela joined in, "Both could lead to death."

DJ jumped up, "Why is everyone attacking my work? None of you have lost a father like I have. You won't understand because you haven't suffered a loss like me." He stormed off to the living room. He wanted to grab his coat and leave. *"Somehow, I become the bad guy. Forget the guy who fights refs and other players on the field; no he's a good guy, but I'm a bad guy for trying to save my father!"*

Tameka joined him in the living room, "Hey, honey, we're not against you, but you can't fault people for having opinions. You know I'm not against you. I just believe that changing the past can have devastating consequences for the future and the now."

"I support you in everything you do. Why can't you support me on this?"

Tameka replied, "Honey, I've supported you from day one. What I want is for you to prove me wrong."

"I will."

"Not only prove me wrong, but prove everyone who laughed at you, wrong too. I'm rooting for you." She hugged him tightly. Angela and Chaquille joined them.

Angela said, "Hey guys, we're going to leave. Chaquille needs to be ready for his big meeting tomorrow and we've upset things here."

DJ popped his lips, "Look, you guys don't have to leave. I'm sorry, I stormed off."

Chaquille said, "Never apologize." He walked to the door. "Thanks for the good word."

DJ nodded and put on a fake smile. Angela hugged Tameka and DJ. "Thanks for dinner, guys. I appreciate it so much."

Tameka said, "You're welcome. I'll call you tomorrow."

The couple left and DJ sat on the couch. He sighed and looked up at Tameka. She did not fully believe in his dream, but she supported him in trying to achieve it. She sat beside him and gave him another hug. DJ said, "You know, in another life, you're probably a leader of people. You know how to get everyone right."

Tameka said, "I do, don't I." She laughed, "I can see myself as a general or something."

DJ laughed with her. "Can you lead us upstairs, General James?"

"I'd be more than happy to, baby."

Chapter 4

Morning rose quick for the Jameses. DJ sipped on his morning coffee while he listened to the shower running upstairs. *"That woman uses more water showering than anyone I know."* DJ picked up the paper and skimmed through it. He landed on more talk about his theories and how the community laughed at him. He blew them off and continued to the sports section.

DJ chuckled at the remarks made by former teammates of Chaquille. *"I can't believe they are still talking about this man. Let it go, he's out of the league now."*

Tameka interrupted his thoughts. She kissed him on the lips, "Don't forget to the call the principal this morning. Chaquille's meeting is at 11."

"I got it on my things to do list, baby."

"Great, I'm out of here, honey."

"Nothing for breakfast?"

"No, I'll grab a Danish or something."

She hurried out of the house while DJ continued to read the newspaper. He looked at his watch and realized he needed to call the principal. He tried to put it off, but went ahead and called. He pulled out his cell and dialed the number, but there was a knock at the door. *"Saved!"*

He rushed to the door. Jeff walked inside, "What's up, man?"

"Hey, good morning, Jeff. I'll be right down. I have to make this phone call to the school that I don't want to make."

"For your brother-in-law? I know you hate that."

"You got it." Jeff went to the basement while DJ called the principal. "Good morning, Principal Giambi. How are you today?"

"I'm doing well, DJ. It's good to hear from our favorite scientist."

"Oh, I don't know if you want me to be your favorite. My colleagues are laughing at me right now."

"They said Einstein's theories were totally impractical. Look at them now."

"Got you. I have to die first." He laughed, but the principal did not laugh. "Sorry, that was in poor taste."

"I believe your theories will be proved. Ironically, it will take time."

"Yes, ironically. You know why I'm calling, right?"

DJ heard Principal Giambi sigh. "Yes, I do. After reviewing the tape of the Miami incident, I can't say I'm going to hire him. I don't need my students exposed to that kind of anger."

"I understand, but he says he's not that guy anymore."

"So, he says."

DJ chuckled to himself, "He did, and I have no love for the guy, but he's my brother-in-law. I can say that I haven't witnessed his temper in person."

"DJ, I will sit down with him and have a discussion. I will consider what you have said and make my decision. I can't promise you anything."

"That's all I can ask."

"Great, when will you come speak to our class again?"

DJ perked up. He loved talking to the kids. "I can come next week."

"Awesome. I will let Mr. Taylor know."

"Great. I can't wait to come out." He hung up the phone and headed to the basement with Jeff.

Jeff looked up from his computer, "Through lying?"

DJ laughed, "You got jokes, my man."

"Look, I think we have something here." DJ looked at the calculations on the computer. He continued, "They are all around us but so small we can't see them, right?"

"Right, but we knew that already."

"Okay, we need an extreme amount of energy to make one big enough to travel through."

DJ sighed, "Again, not something we didn't already know, my friend."

Jeff continued, "So what if we use the same theory in the movie Stargate and build a gate to establish a wormhole?"

DJ snickered, "And they laughed at me."

"No listen, man."

"Jeff, how are we going to get to another planet to put the other gate? Also, how would that get us back in time?"

"We don't go to another planet. We build another one in Europe. Then we use the two to travel back in time."

"How?"

"Remember the episode where the team travelled back to 1964?"

DJ answered, "Yeah, because of the solar…" DJ's mind jumped to where Jeff's mind already was. "You're right. We can use the power of the solar flare to travel back in time." He thought some more, "Wait, we don't know the first thing about building a stargate."

Jeff smiled, "We don't, but I know your boss, Tony Radford, and he's a genius at building scientific things. He helped build rockets for the apollo missions."

"Awesome. Reach out to him and let's talk."

"I already did. He wants to meet at 12."

DJ smiled, "I can't believe it, man. We can do this."

***

DJ and Jeff arrived at the café to meet Tony. It excited DJ to talk about the possibility of traveling through time. Jeff said, "Hey, Tony, how are you, man?"

"I'm good, bro."

Jeff continued, "Remember DJ? You hired him a few years back."

Tony shook hands with DJ. Tony said, "Yes, so you're the man the science community is laughing at and an employee of mine."

"That would be me."

"Look, man, I don't disagree with you. I believe time travel can be conquered."

DJ replied, "Great, then we don't have to fight about it."

Tony laughed, "No, sir. We don't. What's your idea?"

DJ pointed to Jeff. Jeff answered, "Have you seen the show Stargate?"

Tony laughed, "What scientist hasn't?"

Jeff continued, "We can build two gates, one on this continent and the other one in Europe. Then we can open a wormhole from one to the other one but ensure the pathway goes through a solar flare. The same as the 1964 episode."

Tony looked at both of them, "Do you know how much it will cost to build two working gates like the ones in that show? Not to mention the complicated code and power consummation. Also, if I remember correctly, you can't have two gates on the same planet."

DJ added, "There was an episode about the Aschen in which they created travel from one place to another on the planet. We can look at it that way."

Tony replied, "The cost will be in the billions, man. It's not workable."

DJ felt rejected again. His hopes were riding high on the possibility of going back to save his father from becoming a reality. Now those hopes appeared smashed. Tony continued, "You both know it takes an enormous amount of power to create a wormhole. Then you need to introduce particles into the wormhole to make it stable for human travel. We all agree there, right?"

DJ and Jeff both agreed. Tony said, "Then we should use the show Sliders as our example. Familiar with it?"

DJ said, "Yes, it wasn't as good as Stargate, but it was okay."

Tony responded, "That show used a computer to create the wormhole and introduce exotic matter into it. The exotic matter allowed humans to travel through the wormhole to another planet in an alternate universe."

DJ replied, "I get it, but both are theories. We have tried to put together the calculations to create a wormhole, but failed."

Jeff said, "The problem with trying to enlarge a wormhole is knowing where it will be before it starts. All of our test have failed. That's why we're moving to the theory of creating a man-made wormhole. Creating the code and getting the power necessary will be an issue, no matter what we do."

DJ replied, "Look, the power requirements will be enormous, and we won't be able to do it from my home. If we can get a working model, then maybe Sci-Tech will let us attempt it at their facility."

Tony nodded his head in disbelief, "I don't think that will happen. Those guys will do everything in their power to prevent time travel."

DJ asked, "Why do you say that?"

Tony answered, "Think of it from their perspective; would you want the world to change if you're a multi-million dollar corporation?"

"It won't change. I'm just saving my dad."

Jeff replied, "You don't know if saving your dad will change the world or not."

"Come on, Jeff. Let's not do that again. Let's figure out how to do it and where we will get the power."

Both Jeff and Tony nodded in agreement. DJ left the meeting pleased he had two friends to help him with this project, but disappointed that they had no solution to the problem.

After the meeting, DJ realized he did not eat anything. He pulled into a small café in a shopping center near his home. *"Hmm, Stagnum Ignis Shopping Center, I haven't seen this shopping center before. I hope this café is decent. I'm starved."*

DJ walked into the café, and no customers were sitting in the seating area. A young woman greeted him, "Welcome to Lago de Fuego. Will you be dining alone?"

"Yes, no one but me."

"Great. You can have a seat anywhere."

"Thank you. I'll sit here by the wall."

"Great choice. Here's your menu. Can I get you something to drink?"

"I'll just have a glass of water and a chipotle chicken, avocado melt with fries."

"You got it."

"Thanks." DJ sat back in the booth and sighed. Thinking about the conversation with Jeff and Tony made his head spin. The answer always seems close, but flies away. He closed his eyes and envisioned arriving at the precise moment to save his father from the man who killed him.

DJ often wished he could have gotten revenge on the man, but cocaine took that opportunity. When DJ was 16, he watched a story on the news about a man who police found dead in his apartment because of an overdose. When they showed the picture, DJ shivered. It was the man who changed his life forever. Fate took him away, and he never accounted for killing DJ's father.

DJ waited for his food to arrive. A tall, athletic man approached his table. "Good afternoon, sir. How are you enjoying your service?"

"It's great so far. I'm still waiting for my food, but I have nothing to complain about."

"Great, my name is Di A. Blo. Don't laugh. My mother named me Di because she was into chemistry. I was the second son and, well… enjoy your meal."

DJ laughed inside. The man's story was funny. Some mothers should never name their kids. The food arrived and DJ enjoyed his meal. *"That sandwich was the best I ever had. I have to come back here."* He got into his car and drove home to work on his calculations. Hopefully, he would find the answer he needed to save his father.

DJ did not know how long he sat at his computer before Tameka startled him. "Dude, I've been standing here looking pretty, if I say so myself, and you never looked up from that computer."

"Sorry, baby. I've been trying to get this Einstein-Rosen bridge opened. I started the day with excitement, but both ideas we had just seem impossible to happen without major backing."

Tameka hugged him. "You know you have my support, but baby, maybe this isn't something that's possible." DJ looked perplexed. Tameka continued, "Look, I know you wished your dad was still alive, but maybe going back to save him will cause more problems. Maybe God is stopping you at every turn because you shouldn't change fate."

DJ sighed, "Now you? Everyone has turned on me. My mom barely speaks to me now, and now you're turning on me."

"DJ look, I support you. However, what if you change the past and the present is worst? Have you even considered the consequences of your actions?"

"Tameka, sweetheart, my dad was just a scientist in a small lab. He was not the president of the United States, or Einstein. He was just a scientist that nobody even remembers, except me."

Tameka sat down, "You only knew him for the first five years of your life. You don't know what he was into or what he would have done over the last 25 years. Your father could have become president for all we know."

"But what you're saying is my father could be the bad man, and if I save him, the world would be a worse place because of some evil he did. I can't believe you're saying this, Tameka. I'm going to get a drink." DJ headed out the house.

Tameka said, "DJ… DJ come back!"

He did not listen. DJ headed to his car and drove to the Bel Air Lounge for a drink. He was angry and tried to process his wife's words.

DJ arrived at the bar and took a seat at the end. Trina, his favorite bartender, was on shift. "DJ, what's up, bro?"

"Nothing; nothing at all, Trina."

"What will you have?"

"The usual, rum and coke neat."

"You got it." Trina walked away and grabbed his drink. She returned, "Here you go. Let me know if you need anything else."

DJ nodded and took a sip of his drink. He stared at the people in the bar, wondering if any of them mattered in the grand scheme of the world. He asked himself the question that everyone else asked. *Would saving his father send the world spiraling down to a worse condition than it currently is?'* He was sure the answer was no. In his mind, his father was not that important.

He continued to stare into his drink, wondering if his work was worthwhile. For years, he tried to discover time travel. He became the laughingstock of the scientific community and his friends, even though they helped him, didn't believe it could work. Now his wife, the woman he loves, doesn't believe it would work as well. She even went to the point of telling him it would destroy the world.

Now he's sitting in this bar alone, no one believing his theory, no one believed saving his father was a good thing. The song *'After the Love is Gone'* played in the background and pounded his ears. He wondered if he had lost his wife because of his obsession. DJ thought, *"I can't lose her. I have to go back and apologize, but I still have to figure out a solution to time travel. I have to save my dad."* DJ left the bar and headed home. He hoped to make up with Tameka.

DJ noticed the light was about to change and sped up. He got into the intersection. There was a loud crash. He felt the car lift off the ground and flip over several times. He did not know what exactly happened. All he heard were voices shouting in the background.

***

DJ woke up. He must have dozed off after feeling the car lift off the ground. Glancing at his body he realized he must have been dreaming again. He eased down the stairs and into the basement. Taking a seat at his workstation he looked at some numbers. Nothing came to him. *"The answer is here; I know it. I just need to find it. Daddy, I'm going to save you no matter what."*

An hour later he heard Tameka say, "DJ, come to bed, please."

DJ turned. Tameka's silhouette stood poised on the bottom step. Even in the dark, she was the prettiest woman he ever seen in his life. "I'm…" He started to say he would stay for a while longer, but changed his mind. "I'm coming right up, baby." If she came down to ask him to come to bed, she wanted their argument to be over; so, did he.

Tameka hugged him and planted a kiss on his lips. "You know, my aunt says that we should never go to bed with an unresolved issue. I'm sorry for the way I talked to you earlier."

"I'm sorry too, baby."

"I still believe you should stop this pursuit, but if you want to continue it, I'll support you."

He did not like that she wanted him to stop searching for the solution, but at least she would support him. "Thank you for your support, Tameka, but I can't let this go."

She sighed and headed upstairs. DJ followed behind her, admiring her body. Their relationship started when they were kids, but he never stopped admiring her body.

In the bedroom, Tameka asked, "How much longer are you going to continue to search for a solution?"

"As long as it takes."

She sighed again, "DJ, this needs to stop. I've supported you for years, but Jeff makes a great point. Changing the past could have irreparable results."

"Here we go."

"You know what? I'm not talking about this tonight. Let's just go to sleep."

"Dang, sleep! I was hoping for a little more."

"I have a headache."

DJ chuckled. He knew she did not have a headache. She was annoyed that he won't stop. He said, "I don't understand why this sudden change in attitude. You were on my side one hundred percent before today. What happened?"

"I told you, Jeff's comments. You may not believe that saving your father could have effects on the entire world as we know it, but we believe it has to be considered. You're blinded by your passion to save your father, and to you, nothing else matters."

"Everything matters to me, sweetheart, but this is something I have worked all my life. I know it can work, but others have to believe in me, too." Tameka sighed. "Even if you don't believe in me, Tameka, I'll still love you, but I have to finish what I started."

Tameka caressed him tightly. He felt the love she had for him. She said, "What if saving your father causes us to never be together?"

"We talked about that baby. Nothing can stop us from being together."

Tameka released him and looked at him. He recognized the fake smile on her face. She had given this some thought, and now she was hurting. She said, "Baby, those are good words to speak when you're in love but when reality seems to inch closer, don't you have to ask yourself is that true?"

"Tameka—"

"Wait, I'm not done. After your father passed, my mother and your mother connected on a level they never connected on. That's what brought you and I together. I was there for you through all your tears. We grew up together and somewhere along the way we fell in love. We lost our virginity together. Our first kiss was with each other; all of our firsts were with each other."

DJ added, "Our first and only."

"Yes, baby, first and only. But you see, that was all because of the death—sorry to use that word… but the death of your father. If that doesn't happen, they don't connect, and we don't fall in love."

She had a point, and he could not argue with it. All of his life he spent learning to become a scientist and explore time travel. Now he was closer than ever, but still miles away. Could he quit? He could find the solution, go back, and ensure he meets the love of his life. Now he had two missions. DJ replied, "I can't argue with that except to say that I truly believe our love was meant to be. Regardless of the circumstances, I think you and I would be together. Who knows, saving my dad could still cause our moms to connect over the attempt to murder my dad? I have to still try, honey."

Tameka rolled over in the bed and drifted off to sleep. DJ stared at her for a while, then drifted off to sleep himself. It would be another tumultuous sleep for him, worse than any night before. Dreams of death and destruction were everywhere. He found himself in the middle of a cobblestone street crying out for help, but none was forthcoming.

Chapter 5

DJ woke from his sleep in a cold sweat. *"God, what's happening to me? I've never slept like that before."* He got up and headed into the shower. The warm water felt good against his body. *"Where did my lovely bride go? I hope she's not still mad at me."*

DJ dressed and headed downstairs. "No smell of coffee or breakfast."

He picked up the note on the counter and it read, *"DJ, I am having serious issues with this time travel thing you want to do. I'm scared, DJ, and I have to be honest with you. It's hard to support you. I went to visit your mom. Maybe she can make me make sense of all this. Love T."*

Her words cut like a knife into his soul. If he could read between the lines, he would believe she was preparing to leave him. Now he faced losing his wife or saving his father. He could stop his mission to discover time travel and keep his wife. Better yet, he could do his work when she was not around and have both her and his work. He tried Tameka's cell, but she did not pick up. He called his mom's house, "Hey, mom. Is Tameka there?"

"I'm doing fine, son, and how are you?"

He laughed, "I'm good, mom. Sorry, but Tameka's note has me on edge."

"She's right here."

The phone went silent, then she answered, "Hey, DJ. I take it you got my note?"

"I did, and I wasn't happy to read it either."

"DJ, this is eating you up, and it's hard being supportive of something I can't accept. Grief is difficult, but we can endure it. You haven't completely grieved because you think you can fix it. You need to see someone."

DJ could not believe his ears. She was now telling him to see a psychologist. "You can't be serious, honey. I will not see a shrink." His concern over their marriage now became anger. "You don't understand because you've never lost anyone. I thought you loved me." DJ hung up the phone and pounded it on the counter. An act he immediately regretted. *"Dang, what am I doing? Is she right? Should I give this all up and just go on with my life?"*

DJ sat down at his computer and stared at it. He wanted to crunch more numbers, but he could not get his mind off Tameka. *"I shouldn't have hung up on her."* His phone rang. It was Tameka. He picked it up and answered, "Hello, and before you get started, I'm sorry for hanging up on you."

"You should be. This is getting out of hand and it's coming between us. I'm wondering if we shouldn't take a break."

"A break? You mean separate?" She did not respond. DJ continued, "Tameka, I'll stop. I will stop searching for a way to time travel. I can't lose you."

"DJ, that sounds great, but you will always look back and blame me for not pursuing your dream. I don't know if I can live with that. We need to take a break so you can focus totally on your research."

DJ's world was ending. He needed to do something, and fast. "Baby, my research is important to me, but the more I work on it, the more I realize that time travel may be impossible. We're breaking up over something I will never be able to achieve. Let's not do this. Come home and let's talk."

"Are we going to talk or are we going to talk?"

He laughed with her, "Talk using our voices, then maybe some body language later."

Tameka giggled, and he loved hearing that sound. Tameka said, "I'm at work now, but I will come home tonight, and we can talk."

"I'll be waiting, sweetheart."

"Have a great day, DJ."

"You too, honey." He hung up the phone, happy he saved his marriage for now, but what was he going to do about his dad? He did not know how he was going to give up on the one motivation he had all his life; but it was that or lose the love of his life.

DJ did not realize how much time rolled by before. His phone rang. "Hey man, what's up?"

"I'm outside. I tried knocking and ringing the doorbell."

"Jeff, man, I'm sorry. I'm on my way up." DJ ran upstairs and let Jeff inside. "Man, I'm giving up my quest to discover time travel."

"What? How did that decision come about?"

"Tameka. She's been on a roll the last 24 hours saying if I discovered it and used it to save my dad, it could have catastrophic consequences. I don't agree with that, but she's willing to leave me over it. That, I can't live with."

Jeff asked, "Have you read Ecclesiastes, three-one?"

"I can't say that I have, but I'm sure you're going to share it with me."

"Man, just because we're scientist doesn't mean we don't serve God. Science can explain most of the world, but there are things that science can't explain. We, as scientists, won't accept the unexplained."

"I certainly have a difficult time believing in the supernatural. I mean, if God existed, why allow my dad, a good man, to die?"

Jeff sighed, "In Ecclesiastes it says, 'There is a time for everything, and a season for every activity under the Heavens.' That means, and forgive me when I say it, but everything has a time and for your dad, that was his time. We won't know why, but God knows the why. It's not up to us to change that." DJ did not respond. Jeff's words hurt him, but there was a part that believe it could be true.

"Okay, man, we can have this philosophical conversation another day. I need to get ready for my beautiful wife. I'm taking her to Tiffani's off the water. She loves the water and Tiffani's is her once a year restaurant."

"Wow, you must really be in the doghouse."

"Yes, I am. Anyway, I guess we can talk about all this tomorrow, but I feel we are close to a breakthrough man."

Jeff's head snapped back, "I thought you weren't pursuing time travel any longer because of Tameka?"

"Technically I'm not openly pursuing time travel. I will have to create a lab somewhere else, but I can't give up my dream totally. I just need to be on the down low with it. I can't lose my heart."

Jeff laughed, "Theoretically, you can discover time travel and go back in time and to save your marriage."

DJ laughed outwardly, but inside he liked the idea. If he continued his work despite what Tameka said, he could always go back to a point where they are still together and never break up. He said, "Time travel opens the door to many possibilities, my friend."

"Which is why it is not to be pursued."

"I can handle it."

"But you don't know why your father was taken from you. You don't know what it is he would have done if he lived. That unknown variable could be deadly."

"I'll take that risk."

Jeff sighed, "But you can't for the rest of the world." He walked out of the basement, leaving DJ to his own thoughts. He quickly dismissed Jeff's comments and headed to the bedroom to get dressed for dinner.

DJ got dressed and looked at his watch. It was near seven and Tameka was not home. He dialed her number, but it went straight to voicemail. A few minutes later, Tameka walked through the door. DJ looked into her eyes and he noticed something he had not seen before. "Where were you?"

"At dinner. I needed some time to think about our future."

"I told you I was giving up time travel."

"I can't let you do that."

"Were you with someone else?"

"Why would you ask me that, DJ?"

"The look in your eyes. I've never seen that look before. Is this the first time?"

"I haven't been out with anyone. I was by myself, but someone introduced themselves to me." She placed her purse on the counter and sighed, "I let him sit with me and for the first time I saw him differently. It was nice talking to someone who wasn't engulfed in something so much that they can't see the love I have for them."

"You love him?"

"No, but you see my point. He was focused on me; nothing else."

DJ felt a pit in his stomach. "Don't leave me, Tameka. I've given up my search for time travel. I was prepared to take you to Tiffani's tonight. I wanted the next chapter to start with a great dinner at your favorite place."

Tameka smiled, "Are you sure you will not look back with regret?"

DJ grabbed her by the shoulders, "I'm not, baby. The only regret I would have is if I let my obsession cause me to lose you." DJ hugged Tameka, but that pit in his stomach would not go away. He left God's bosom years ago, but now he silently prayed to Him.

"Let me be transparent with you, DJ." The pit grew inside his stomach. "I wanted to go home with him, but my mother didn't raise me to be that woman. I never wanted to be that woman." DJ popped his lips. He could not hold back the tears and they rushed down his face. She continued, "Remember when my dad came home and found my mom in the bed with another man?"

"I do."

"I vowed that day I would not be that woman. Now, I'm glad I kept that vow. You have your chance, DJ, but if you go back to the obsession, I will leave."

"I will not go back to it. Tomorrow I will go to the school and apply for a teaching position. Principal Giambi has been trying to get me onboard since I became the laughingstock of the science community."

Tameka smiled and hugged him again. This time, it felt like the first time. It felt like she loved him, and he loved her. Inside, he did not want to give up searching for a way to go back and save his dad, but the close brush with losing Tameka was a true wakeup call. He would give it up.

DJ guided her up the stairs and to their bedroom. He made love to her on more occasions than he could count, but tonight would be the one that would restart their marriage. He removed her clothing piece by piece and met with no resistance. She wanted him as much as he wanted her. He laid her down in the center of their king size bed and kissed her gently on the lips, making his way down her body.

**

DJ woke the next morning with Tameka in his arms. He smiled as he stared at her. He whispered, "I love you so much. You're my world." Tameka smiled, letting him know she heard him. "So, you're not asleep?"

"Nope. I'm just enjoying every moment before I have to go to work."

"Can I ask you a question?"

She turned around and looked him in his eyes. "It was Evan. I never knew that side of him, but I'm still committed to you and only you."

"How did you know what I was referring to?"

"I'm your wife. I know everything." She got up and headed to the shower. She shouted, "I love you too, DJ."

DJ fell backwards in the bed. The pit in his stomach was completely evaporated. The love he had for Tameka returned. His cell rang. "Hey Jeff, why are you up so early in the morning?"

"Are we continuing our work? Tony offered me a job at his company. I told him if our work was over, I would take it."

"Our work is over, man. I almost lost Tameka last night."

Jeff gasped, "Really? What happened?"

"She had more than enough of my obsession. I didn't realize how much she was fed up, until last night. She says it was your words about time travel that made her feel that way, but I think it was brewing for a while. Your words probably brought it to the surface."

"Sorry, man. If I knew she would react that way, I wouldn't have said anything."

"It's not your fault. I've been neglecting her, and I won't do that anymore. From now on, Tameka is the priority."

"Cool, man. Let me call Tony."

"Congratulations, Jeff."

"What are you going to do for work?"

"I'm going to work at the high school. I don't need a ton of money, so it will do for now. Besides, I love inspiring minds."

"Great. I'm sure they can't wait to hire you."

"That's for sure. Enjoy your day, man."

"Thanks, DJ. You do the same."

DJ hung up the phone. Tameka came out of the bathroom in her robe, drying her hair. "Who was that?"

"Jeff. He wanted to make sure we were done before he accepted another job."

Tameka said, "So you are serious about quitting?"

"I am, baby."

"Where's he working?"

"Radford Technology. He knows the boss, so it was easy."

"Cool. What time are you going to the school?"

"After you go to work. I'll follow you out."

Tameka replied, "Sounds like a plan."

"Great, I'll go make us some coffee. Do you want breakfast?"

"Some pancakes would be nice, babe."

"You got it, Tameka, the love of my life." They both laughed and DJ headed downstairs. He gathered the items to make pancakes and started brewing the coffee.

Tameka came down the steps, "Whoa, that smells good baby."

"Anything for you, love."

She planted a kiss on his lips. "Make my plate?"

"Absolutely baby." DJ grabbed a couple of plates and placed them on the table. "Here you go, sweetheart." They sat down to breakfast and DJ's world felt repaired.

They enjoyed breakfast and headed out to their respective destinations. On the drive, DJ's thoughts about his father and what life would have been like filled his mind. *"I need to stop thinking about that and focus on what I have before me. I think I'll buy us tickets to Cancun. She will love Mexico!"*

DJ diverted his destination to Orange Hill Cemetery, where his father was buried. He wanted to tell him he would not be going back in time to save him.

The long walk across the cemetery seemed to take hours, but it did not bother him. He reached the familiar headstone and brushed off the leaves. DJ knelt down to get closer to his dad. *"Daddy, you know I have spent every day trying to go back and save you. But, dad, I can't anymore. My wife, Tameka, you knew her when she was 8, but it was your death that brought us closer together. I can't lose her dad, so I have to give up searching for the answer. Dad, wherever you are, I hope you are good and smiling down on my decision. Well, I have to go to the high school and become a science teacher. Take care, daddy."*

DJ left the graveyard. He jumped into his car and sped off. He continued to worry that Tameka would leave him for Evan. *"It was close this time, but the longer I focus on time travel, the greater my chance of losing my wife."* Other men always approached Tameka and none of them were obsessed with traveling back in time.

DJ arrived at Dr. Martin Luther King High School. The principal, Selena Giambi, was a childhood friend and she wanted him to teach at the school for years. DJ walked into her office, where she was deep into her computer. DJ said, "Good morning, Selena."

"DJ, good morning. How are you?"

"I'm good, sort of."

"Well, what brings you to King High?"

"A job."

"Excuse me?"

DJ could not believe he was uttering the words, but to save his marriage, he needed to say them. "I'm giving up the search for time travel and returning to the classroom. I don't want to teach at the college level right now, so… do you have a job?"

"I do, my science teacher quit, so Mr. Spellman and Mrs. Daniels will be happy to turn it over to you."

DJ smiled, "They don't want to teach science?"

"They aren't science teachers. One teaches physical education, and the other teaches English. They were filling in since we didn't have a science or biology teacher."

"Great, so when do I start?"

"How about tomorrow?"

"I'll be here. Thanks, Selena. I won't let you down."

Selena asked, "So, why did you quit your research?"

"Well, my research became my obsession. It was something I worked on day and night. So much that I stopped paying attention to my wife. Once she threaten to leave me for another man, it became official. I needed to quit my marriage or quit my research. I left my research."

"The woman has power, woo hoo! I can certainly understand her position. Frankly, I'm happy you made the choice you made. Your wife is a good woman. Time travel is something you may never figure out. In fact, it's something I believe is impossible." DJ looked down. "Hey, I'm not laughing at you. I supported your research, but I don't believe it's possible. Some things are left to God and when man tries to intervene, it can destroy us."

"I'm not a supporter of God. Where was He when my dad was killed?"

"I can't answer that question, DJ, but as a Christian woman, I know nothing happens in God's world by accident. It may be painful for us to lose someone, but there is a reason. Going back and changing time means changing God's grand plan. That can't be good for the world."

DJ felt the anger rise inside, but he did not want his new boss to know it. "Well, thanks for the advice. I'll see you tomorrow morning."

"I'll be here. Come in here first and Rachel will help you with your hiring paperwork."

"Will do. Thank you." DJ walked out of her office and to his car. He sat behind the wheel and looked out over the parking lot. "Why does everyone think I need to be preached to? I lost my father at five years old and now everyone is telling me about God. If you're out there, God, Jesus… why didn't you save my dad?"

DJ's car sped out of the parking lot. He drove to get himself something to eat.

DJ arrived at his now favorite restaurant and was led to his favorite booth. He sat down and ordered the usual. The owner approached him and took a seat across from him. This time, he looked very different. He had a jet black goatee and slick back hair. His finely tailored Navy blue suit fit him perfectly. DJ admired his dress and personal appearance. He asked, "You look like the owner, but you've changed. Who are you, and where did you come from?"

"I am the owner, but I am also the man who can help you solve your problem."

DJ squirmed in his seat. "Um, what problem is that?"

The man smiled, "Do we really need to go through all this? We both know the biggest issue you need solved in your life, and I'm here to help you solve it."

DJ chuckled, "Look man, I don't know who you are but I'm just here for a quick sandwich, then I'll need to get back home. I don't have time for this. Who put you up to it? Jeff… Tony? One of the scientists laughing at me?"

"No one put me up to it." The man leaned forward, "I just want to help you."

The server arrived with the food. DJ said, "Miss, can I get this to go?"

"Sure, sir. I'll be right back."

DJ replied, "Thank you."

The man said, "Why don't you eat here with me?"

"Like I said, I need to get back home and frankly, I'm not comfortable right now."

"Of course, you're not. You're used to solving your own problems. You're a scientist and you believe that all nature's issues are scientific in creation." DJ looked at the man, but each time he focused on him, DJ quickly looked away. The man continued, "But fortunately, your problem can be solved with science, just not the science you're familiar with."

DJ was getting intrigued. The woman returned. "Here you go, sir."

"Thank you." DJ handed her the money. "You can keep the change." He looked at the man, "Thank you for the conversation. Take care."

The man grabbed him by the arm, "Here, take my card. When you become frustrated enough, contact me. I will tell you how to solve your problem."

"Are you a scientist?"

"No, but I have information that can help you."

DJ sighed, "Yeah, um, take care. He looked at the card, Mr. Diablo? What kind of name is that?"

"Spanish… call me when you're ready to travel back to save your father."

The man walked away, leaving DJ standing by the table, stunned at the man's words. *Who is that guy and how does he know so much about me?* DJ returned to his car and drove home. He sat in the driveway eating his food and contemplating Diablo's words. DJ blew off the man and returned to the basement to crunch some numbers. He wanted to track the micro wormholes, hoping to enlarge one of them. If he could calculate where the next one would open, enlarge it, and introduce the black matter particles into it, he could go back and save his dad, all before Tameka came home.

The time rolled by quickly, and DJ rushed upstairs hoping Tameka wouldn't catch him. She came through the door, and they embraced. He asked, "You know I have to ask."

"Nothing happened. I told him what I said at dinner was wrong and that I love you. I hurt his feelings."

"To bad."

"DJ, be nice."

"Be nice? He was pushing up on my wife. I can't be nice to a guy like that. He should respect the bounds of marriage."

"You're right, he should, but I shouldn't have led him on. Can we change the subject?"

"Sure."

"How did it go at school?"

"I got preached to, but I got the job as well."

"Awesome! I am so happy, DJ. Now we can live a regular life. Let's go celebrate."

"Where?"

"Tiffani's. You were going to take me there yesterday."

"Sounds good. Let me shower and change."

She pushed past him and ran upstairs shouting, "Me first!"

He laughed. Life was returning to normal. His wife was happy again and in the grand scheme of things that mattered the most.

After a great dinner and a romantic night, DJ found himself in a deep sleep.

Chapter 6

Morning rose faster than normal. DJ's body felt like it was still asleep, but he got himself up and showered. Eventually he headed out to work.

DJ's first day at King High was busy filling out paperwork and getting familiar with his new students. Most of them wanted to hear his theories on time travel. He hated the internet. You can find anything on the internet, and they found him.

During lunch, he decided to get away. Down the street from the school was Lago de Fuego. Mexican sounded good and it was quick. As good as the food was, he never understood why no one was there.

He arrived and the host sat him at the same table. He ordered the usual meal and checked his personal email on his phone. The door chimed letting him know someone entered the establishment. It was Diablo. *"That guy knows I'm here every time I come."*

Diablo sat down and motioned to the server. "My friend, DJ. How is life in your mundane job?"

"Life is fine. My marriage has turned around. We're even talking about having a baby."

"So wonderful. Most cannot overcome infidelity."

"My wife didn't cheat on me."

"So you say, but have you considered my offer? I can take you to an abyss at the edge of the universe. There, you will find the answer to time travel."

DJ laughed, "Dude, the edge of the universe? That's a farce. What does it even mean, anyway?"

Diablo looked deep into DJ's eyes. A chill ran up and down DJ's spine. Diablo said, "It is not a farce. Come with me and I will show you how to change the world." DJ hesitated again. "What have you got to lose? If I'm wrong, you will continue to live your chosen path, but if I am correct, you can save your father and return to this life knowing time travel is possible with the supernatural."

DJ thought about the offer. What could he lose by going with him? If he was the crackpot DJ thought he was, then he would only lose a few minutes of his day. But if he was correct, and the supernatural is the way to solve time travel, he could save his dad and keep his wife.

DJ said, "How do we get there?"

Diablo smiled, "I will come to you at midnight and take you to the sphere. You must be asleep for the journey, for no one but me can know its location."

"At midnight?"

"At midnight, come outside of your home. I will be there waiting."

DJ said, "Okay, I will be there."

Diablo stood and buttoned his coat. "You will not regret your decision."

DJ already regretted it. Something did not sit right with him, but if there was an opportunity to have his wife and save his father, he had to take it even if he did not believe in the supernatural.

He finished his food and returned to work. The kids and their antics took his mind off Diablo for the rest of the school day. On the drive home, he could not think of anything else. When he pulled into the driveway and went inside, he was met by Tameka. "You forgot, didn't you?"

"What?"

"You were supposed to bring dinner."

"Oh, goodness. I'm so sorry. Those kids worked every nerve I have. I'll run back out."

"Don't bother, but you can take me out again." He grinned, "That's the price you pay for forgetting your wife."

DJ quickly replied, "I will never forget my wife. I might have forgotten dinner, but there's no way I forgot Tameka James." She smiled at him and squeezed his cheek. Then she kissed him. "How can a man forget something so special as you?"

"I don't know, Mr. James, but you did forget to feed me."

They continued their banter to dinner and throughout the evening. The closer it came to midnight, the more DJ worried. He constantly asked himself, was he doing the right thing or not? The answer kept coming up 'yes' he was.

It was two minutes to midnight. He got up and looked at Tameka. He silently prayed she would not wake up and catch him sneaking out.

She didn't wake up. He tipped out the room and down the stairs. DJ turned off the alarm and eased out the front door. He paused at the sight of a blood red Corvette waiting for him on the street. Diablo stood by the driver's side door with a smirk on his face.

DJ asked himself one final time if he was ready and the answer came back 'yes' again. He walked up to Diablo. Diablo asked, "Are you prepared to enter the world of the supernatural?"

"I guess I am."

"There's no guessing. Either you are or you are not. We dislike lukewarm people."

"I am ready."

"Get in, my friend." DJ got inside the car. He glanced upstairs and saw a figure in his home. That pit in his stomach returned. She saw him leave so he would have to deal with questions when he returned. Diablo continued, "I must put you to sleep, my friend."

"Why can't I know where it is? I will need to find it to return to this time."

"You will not know where to find it in the past. The doorway moves every seven years."

"I see. How are you going to…" DJ was knocked out in seconds. When he woke, he was in a dark place. Outside the car he saw Diablo talking to creatures. He could not make out what they looked like, but they were not human. He refocused his eyes and they were gone.

DJ stepped out the vehicle and Diablo said, "You are awake. How nice."

DJ asked, "Who were you talking to?"

"No one. You must have been imagining things. The gas can have that effect. Come this way."

DJ saw a large cavern. They walked inside of it. The cave appeared to be hundreds of years old, damp and scary. *"What am I getting into?"* Diablo turned and smiled at him. *"Did he read my thoughts? There's really some stuff going on here."*

Diablo said, "Here." He pointed toward a cliff. There was a large gap between the two sides. "This is where you can travel back in time."

DJ asked, "How, jump off this cliff?"

"Look down the cliff, my friend."

DJ did as he was told. Flashes of history poured through like a roaring stream in a river. He saw Hitler invade Poland. "That was in 1939!"

"Yes, my friend, keep watching. There is more."

DJ was fixed on the events of world history as they unfolded before his eyes. He witnessed the assassinations of Martin Luther King and John F. Kennedy. He saw the Watergate trials. DJ gasped at the history that passed by like a river. He said, "How is this possible?"

Diablo smiled, "Time is like a river. It flows continuously. Some of your scientists' friends got time right. The others, not so much. They only see what they see with their natural eyes. When you open your mind, you realize time moves in all directions.

Events of the past continue to happen and if you jump into the abyss at the right time, you will be there to save your father."

"I'm ready."

"Wait until that time comes, then you jump in. However, there are rules and unfortunately, like anything, they come with a price."

"You didn't mention a price before. I don't have any money on me."

Diablo smiled, "I don't require money. I have all of that I need. What I require is you."

"Me? What does that mean?"

"That means you sign this contract and I own you. When I need something from you, you provide it. It's a simple deal."

"What are the rules?"

Diablo smiled again, "You can only enter the abyss three times. If you enter it a fourth time; well, you will die an instant and horrible death."

"Okay, three times. I only need two."

"Right. You can only go to a point where you are alive. Meaning you cannot travel back to a time before you were born. If you do, you will die an instant and horrible death."

"Okay, I don't need to go back any farther than 25 years. Anymore rules?"

"Last, you can only stay for 48 hours. After 48 hours—"

"I know I will die an instant and horrible death."

"Actually, no. You will cease to exist."

DJ popped his lips, "So, let me get this straight. If I jump in to save my father but I stay longer than 48 hours, I can't get my last two jumps."

"Correct. You can jump three times, but if you stay in the past or the future if you decide to go there, you can only stay for 48 hours. After that, you will cease to exist because two versions of you cannot exist at the same time forever."

"But when I jump back here, I can stay forever?"

"Yes, but here is where you ultimately want to be."

"Okay, but I'm really worried about losing my wife."

"Why? When you return, you will be home in your bed. She will never know you left."

"Are you sure?"

"I'm very sure she won't know anything about you leaving the house."

DJ could not believe what was happening. He had the opportunity to travel back and save his dad while continuing to keep his marriage intact. He asked, "There has to be a catch; this is too perfect."

"This is time travel, my friend. It is the only way it can happen. Mankind will never be able to go back in time, but this abyss is supernatural and doesn't play by your physics rules."

"Let me ask, how can that be? Who built this?"

"You are asking so many questions while your time to jump is approaching." DJ did not respond. Diablo said, "This abyss was created by the first people millions of years ago. They were a race that far exceeded anything your people have done. However, in all their vast technology, they could not give life to the abyss. That could only occur in the supernatural realm."

"Who gave it life?"

"That is beyond your understanding."

"I see."

"Here, sign this agreement and prepare yourself to jump. Your time is approaching."

DJ said, "I need to read it first."

"You don't have time to read it. Your time is approaching. Sign it and read it later."

"Okay, I don't have a…" Before he could finish, Diablo handed him a pen. "Thanks. I feel like I'm signing away my soul." He signed the paper. "Red ink? That's unusual."

"This is the supernatural, my friend. We sign everything in red. It is the currency of the supernatural. Now your time is here. Jump!"

DJ, without preparation, jumped into the abyss. His body felt as though it were pulled in several directions at once. He could see events as they happened all around him. One caught his eye. He saw the day he proposed to Tameka. He was down on one knee at their favorite restaurant asking her to marry him. It was one of the best days of his life. It faded like it never happened.

Then the day they were married flowed past him. His wedding brought a smile to his face. Then it faded. The further he fell, the more history changed. Images of destroyed cities, bodies laid everywhere, some showed signs of disease, while others were murdered. It was like his dream.

DJ's heart dropped when he saw Tameka's death alone on a dark street. Tears flowed down his face.

Chapter 7

DJ's body hit the ground with a thump. He stood to his feet and looked around. It appeared to be the same cavern as before. DJ brushed himself off and walked toward what he thought was the exit. Behind him, the cavern disappeared, and he stood a block away from his old home.

He looked around and couldn't believe his eyes. The cars were 25 years old but looked new. The houses which were run down in his era were like new again. He spotted Diane and her son, Aaron. Aaron was four when DJ's father died. He watched him running around with his mom. At that point, he knew he had travelled back in time.

DJ set his timer on his watch for 47 and a half hours. The time he would have to travel back home. He pulled out his cell to call his house to see if he would get an answer, but nothing worked on it. "I *should have expected to get no reception, since there are no cell towers now. This is amazing, but I need to determine what day it is."*

A neighbor walked out of her home and spotted him standing there. She asked, "Are you lost?"

"I'm a little disoriented. What day is it?"

"June 3rd."

DJ was excited, "I mean, what year is it?"

She looked perplexed. "Are you sure you're, okay?"

"Just humor me, ma'am. What year is it?"

"1998."

DJ clasped his hands together, forming fists, and celebrated. He was back in time, 25 years, and one day prior to the day his father was murdered. He said, "Thank you, ma'am. Thank you so much!" He rushed off, looking for somewhere to spend the night. The next day, he would have to stop the man from killing his father.

DJ made his way to a local tavern and sat at the bar. He realized his ID would cause questions and prayed no one asked him for it. The bartender was around his age, black and beautiful. "Wow, if I didn't have Tameka, I'd surely try her."

The bartender made her way to DJ, "Can I get you something to drink?"

"I'll just have a glass of white wine."

"Coming up."

"Thank you." He was glad she did not ask for his ID.

Halfway into his glass of wine, a man took a seat next to him. He told the bartender, "I'll have the same thing he's having."

"Coming up."

The man smiled at DJ, "My name is Gabriel. What's yours?"

"Derek James, but people call me DJ."

"Hmm, there's a kid on Nautica Place that goes by DJ, and his name is Derek James. He's only five, though."

"You know him?"

"I know him and his family. They are great people."

DJ shook his head because he didn't remember this man. Did he stop coming around after his dad died? Who is he really? "I've never seen you around here. Where do you live?"

"I could do like Diablo and tell you a string of lies until you do what he needs you to do, but I will not do that."

DJ was confused. How does this man know Diablo? "How do you know about him?"

"We go back a long time." DJ was perplexed. "You're here to save your father. I'm here to talk you out of it."

"Do you know how much I have gone through to get here? There's no way I'm going to stop now."

"If you save your father, it will have ramifications you can't fathom."

"I'm not stopping." DJ got up, flung a twenty on the bar, and left. He walked down the street until he came upon a park. He found a bench and took a seat. *"I guess this is where I'm sleeping tonight."*

It was one of those familiar hot summer nights. DJ wasn't used to them since he often stayed in his air conditioned home. He laid down on the bench and tried to get some sleep.

The sleep came quicker than he expected, and the nightmare came with more intensity. He struggled on the bench, tossing and turning in a sweat. Visions of Tameka with Evan in a world that was not familiar to him pounded his mind. In one final intense nightmare, he watched his dad die again, over and over in different ways.

The sun broke through the trees and smacked DJ in the face. He shot up and looked at his watch. The murder occurred at 1:30, so he had six hours to get ready. *"Ugh, a note for time travel. Grab a toothbrush and toothpaste."* He checked his wallet. *"Two twenties, I guess I will eat."* He walked down the street to a café and had a seat. He ordered his breakfast and sipped on his coffee. Minutes later, Gabriel joined him at his table.

"I came off rough last night. Maybe we can start over?"

"If you're here to stop me from saving my father, you can stop because I'm not doing that. I've endured too much and came too far to get to this point."

Gabriel said, "I just want to talk to you about what could happen when you play God."

"Play God? First, you have to believe in God to play God. Second, all my life, my goal was to discover the solution to time travel and save my dad. I didn't discover the solution, but I got here… now I'm going to save my dad. I don't care what the ramifications of that are."

"You really don't care?"

"No, I don't."

"That's a shame." He got up from his seat and looked into DJ's eyes. DJ could see the sadness in his eyes. "If you change your mind, contact me here."

DJ looked at the card. It was the church he attended when he was a kid. "Are you the pastor?"

"No, I just attend." Gabriel walked away.

DJ felt horrible for talking to Gabriel the way he did. He took his time eating breakfast and drinking his coffee. When he was finished, he made his way to the community to scout the area. Most of what he remembered was still in place. He hung out in the woods and waited. From his location, he could see when the man would make his way toward the younger version of him and his father.

DJ sat in the woods wondering what would change with his father in his life. He knew being a scientist would still be his passion because his father held the same passion. He thought he would learn more about science as a child and learn how to fish. Fishing was something he always wanted to learn. He knew his father fished but without him in his life, he never learned.

The appointed time arrived, and DJ made his way to the spot he could cut off the man. DJ saw him talking to another man. They appeared to have a serious discussion. DJ wondered what they were discussing, but blew it off.

The man headed toward the younger DJ. It was about to happen again. DJ cut him off. The man was stunned. He said, "Get out my way dude, I got a job to do."

The comment confused DJ. Was his father assassinated? DJ said, "You're not going anywhere this time."

The man twisted his face, "What are you talking about, dude?" He reached for his gun, but DJ grabbed his arm and wrestled him to the ground. They rolled over and over until the man was on top of DJ. He tried to point the gun at him, but DJ swiped it away.

The man struck DJ twice in the face, but DJ blocked the third one and pushed him to the side. They got up. The man said, "What is your issue, man? I got work to do and you're stopping me."

"What job?"

The man rushed DJ and slammed his shoulder into DJ's stomach. They fell backwards and struggled for the advantage. DJ saw the younger him and his dad come out of the house, get in the car and drive off. *"They, we made it!"* He fought the man off. DJ watched the man run in the opposite direction.

DJ stood to his feet. He picked up the gun and stuck it into his waist. Diablo stood in the woods. DJ walked over to him. "What are you doing here?"

"Just watching to see if you completed your mission."

DJ smiled, "I did it. I stopped my father from being killed."

"Did you?"

"Yes, you saw right?"

"You delayed his murder. Didn't you hear the man say he had a job to do?"

"What does that mean?"

"It means your father's murder wasn't a chance encounter. He was targeted." He pulled out a newspaper article. "Look at the date on this paper."

"It's dated tomorrow, and it says my father still dies."

"Yes, this time at the park where he took you. The same man kills him. The only way you can stop this is to kill that man and his boss."

"His boss? Who is that?"

"Get that out of him, but your father was on to something. Look at this article from last week."

"Prominent scientist close to cure for cancer? This is my dad?"

"The people who want him dead, don't want this cure to come out. It could save millions. You're not just fighting for your dad; you're fighting for millions."

"I'll get to the park."

"You do that." Diablo smiled and DJ ran off. He needed to get to the park and stop the murder.

"I can't believe it. My dad was on to a cure for cancer. I told Tameka and Jeff they were wrong. My dad is a hero."

Out of breath, he made it to the park. In the distance, he saw his dad and his younger self playing on the swings. He spotted the man easing up on them. DJ darted over to him and tackled him to the ground. The gunshot roared into the air and sent the park visitors running in every direction.

DJ continued to wrestle with the man until the gun went off again. This time, the bullet went into his stomach. DJ jumped up. He watched the blood ooze out of the man. He asked him, "Who are you working for?"

The man said, "Why? What are you to them?"

"I am him. Who told you to kill my dad?"

The man looked confused. "Palmer Mason. He paid me fifty thousand to kill him, make it look like a mugging."

"I'll get you some help."

"I'm not going to make it. You can't be his son. His son is five."

"I travelled back in time to save my dad." The man looked more confused as his eyes closed, never to open again.

DJ looked at his watch. Time was counting down. He needed to find Palmer Mason and stop him from hiring another hit man.

DJ searched the man's pockets and found a business card with Palmer Mason's information on it. He put the card in his pocket and ran away from the scene. *"I can't allow myself to be caught. I mean, how can I explain that I'm from the future?"*

DJ had three hours to remain in the past. Palmer Mason's apartment building was on the other side of town, and he had no money to get there. "There's no way I can get there and back in three hours." A car pulled up the curb and DJ felt nervous. He wondered if someone was going to take a shot at him.

The car window came down and the man inside said, "Need a ride, DJ?"

DJ asked, "How do you know my name?"

"I'm a friend of Diablo."

DJ could not understand what was going on. He got inside the car and said, "Diablo sent you to follow me?"

"We look out for our own."

"What does that mean? I don't belong to anyone."

"But you do, my friend. You signed that contract, remember?"

DJ had not thought about the contract since he arrived in the past. He focused on saving his dad. DJ pulled the contract out of his back pocket and read it.

His eyes popped when he read the section that talked about his soul. "Oh, my God!"

The driver laughed, "God? You mean that person you said didn't exist?" He laughed even louder.

"I can't do this."

"Bruh, you already did it. Here's Palmer Mason's building. Handle your business."

"Why does Diablo want this to happen?"

"That's not for you to know. You do your part. That's all you need to know."

"If I don't stop Palmer Mason, then Diablo doesn't get what he wants."

The driver looked at DJ. "That means you're useless to us, but before we kill you, we'll kill your wife. I personally would do more than kill her, but the boss would just want her dead."

DJ's anger rose, "You touch my wife and you're dead."

The driver laughed again, "Go handle your business."

DJ stepped out of the car. Palmer Mason's penthouse was on the top floor. DJ walked inside. The security guard said, "You're here for Palmer?"

DJ's head twisted, "You know?"

The security guard turned the key to get the elevator open. He pushed the button and stepped back. DJ stepped into the elevator and the doors closed. "This is crazy. What have I gotten myself into? I should have listened to my mom and trusted God. The supernatural is real."

DJ made it to the top floor, and the elevator opened. The penthouse took him in awe. The apartment was magnificent. He thought about life with Tameka in that penthouse. Standing by the window was a tall dark skinned man. He stared out the window intently. DJ stopped ten feet from him.

The man said, "I'm Palmer Mason. Diablo sent you, right?"

"Wait, you know this man, too."

Palmer nodded and turned toward DJ, "Who doesn't know the devil?"

"Come on, man. The devil wears a red suit and has horns. That isn't him."

"Man, you have so much to learn. Diablo recruited me ten years ago. He gave me everything I needed to make it to the top. All I needed to do was sign a contract. I was so hungry and desperate I was willing to do anything I could to make it to the top."

DJ wanted to interrupt him, but he did not. He waited for Palmer to gather himself. Palmer continued, "When he found me, I was living on the street. I used to sleep in my car, but I got so hungry I sold it. After that money ran out, I had nothing left. Nothing until he showed himself to me in an alley. He said he could change my life. He gave me a formula to create medicine that could help people with various diseases. One of which was cancer. It wasn't a cure for it, but it will help people deal with the effects of cancer.

DJ said, "Man, that's a deep story."

"There's more. My life boomed. I went from eating scraps to dining in fine restaurants all over the world. My bank account went from zero to eight figures almost overnight. Then a man came out with research that was on track to cure cancer. If his research came through, it would cost me billions. I had to do something about it, so I hired a low-budget hitman to take him out. It was supposed to be a simple hit. Make it look like a mugging and I would get back to making my money. When the hit went sour, Diablo showed up. He said he needed that man to live, and it was time to call in my contract."

"What does that mean?"

Palmer picked up his drink and took a sip. The drink was straight, and his face showed it burned as it went down. He looked at DJ and said, "One piece of advice, get out of the contract." Palmer turned toward the balcony, ran, and jumped off.

DJ rushed to the balcony, hoping to catch him. He looked over. Palmer's body laid on the ground with blood spattered in all directions. DJ sighed and rushed out of the penthouse. He darted into the elevator and headed to the car. The driver smiled at him. "Amazing the power Diablo has over us, isn't it?"

"Why did I need to be there?"

"Isn't it oblivious?"

"No, it's not."

"We all need a lesson in what we signed up for. In case you didn't know, now you do."

DJ did not say another word on the drive. The man drove him to a vacant lot. DJ asked, "Why am I here?"

"You want to go back to your time, right?"

"I do."

"Just wait here for a few minutes. Welcome to the family."

DJ nodded. He did not want to be welcomed. When he arrived back in his time, he hoped to find his wife and parents home enjoying time together. If that would be the case, DJ believed it would have been worth it.

The area around DJ changed. He found himself in the large cavern where his journey back in time began. He looked over the cliff and watched the river of time flow. It was nearing the time when he left, but it looked different. A newspaper flashed across the river with the date on it. It was the date DJ left. He dove into the river and experience the same ripping effect as he did on his first journey. Time moved around him, but the events looked different. They were darker now, more death than before. DJ wondered what had happened. He regretted not listening to Tameka and Jeff.

Again, he hit the ground with a thump. However, this time, he landed at the feet of Diablo. DJ looked up, and Diablo grinned a hideous grin. DJ stood up, "What did you make me do?"

"My friend, I did not make you do anything. You wanted to save your father, and I gave you the opportunity to do just that."

"A man killed himself for you. He did that just for you to prove a point to me. Why?"

"Because you are a scientist. You think all things can be explained through science. You need to learn that the supernatural is where the real power lies and I, my friend, am the most powerful being you will ever meet. I own your soul, you are mine."

"I will find a way out of this, but now I'm going to see my family."

"Go ahead."

DJ stopped and turned around. "How do I get back home?"

Diablo laughed, "Walk through that door."

"That simple?"

"This is the world of the supernatural. Sometimes it is that simple."

DJ walked to the door and grabbed the handle. He looked back, and Diablo hunched his shoulders. DJ turned the knob and walked through the door.

Chapter 8

DJ found himself in a lab coat standing in the hallway of what appeared to be a large building. People were milling about in every direction, focused on whatever task they needed to accomplish. *"Where do I go?"*

A man rushed DJ from behind, "DJ… where have you been? Never mind, I think we've done it, son. We've created a cure for cancer!"

DJ's eyes popped out of his head. He did not hear a word his father said. The joy of seeing his father alive filled his heart more than he realized. He smiled and hugged his dad as hard as he could. Derek Sr. said, "I know, son, I know… now we can honor your mom!"

"Honor mom?"

"Yes, have you forgotten? This was all about honoring your mom and the battle she fought. Now no one will have to suffer as she did. Let's go."

"Suffer as she did? Are you saying mom is dead?"

"Derek Jr., what is wrong with you?"

"I'm not sure, dad, but I'll be okay."

Derek Sr. patted him on the shoulder. They ran out of the hallway and into the laboratory, where other scientists and technicians were standing around. Derek Sr. said, "Everybody, this is a historic day for all of us. We will celebrate this discovery around the world. Millions of people will be healed of that dreaded disease, cancer." The lab exploded with happiness.

DJ summarized many of them had family fighting cancer, but he never knew his mom had it. He needed to find out what had happened to her. How long ago did she die? Did he trade losing one parent for another one? Too many questions for him to answer.

Derek Sr. continued, "I want everyone to take the rest of the day off and celebrate in your own way. We are going to get this cure out to hospitals and start saving people."

DJ asked, "Don't we need FDA approval first?"

"Son, where is your head? The FDA has been involved from the start. Everyone in the world has been waiting for this cure." Derek Sr. turned back to the room, "Don't mind my son, everyone. He seems to be suffering from too much joy today."

Everyone laughed. A couple of technicians patted him on the back as they were leaving. One scientist came up to him, "Great job, DJ. This is going to put both of you in the history books."

DJ grabbed him by the shoulders, "Jeff, man, how are you? You don't know what I've been through, man."

"Um, we don't know each other like that, DJ. Your dad is right. Something is off with you."

"What, dude… we go way back?"

"Way back to last week. I just started working here a week ago."

DJ nodded his head in disbelief. "Look, man, I don't know what's happening here, but I know you and your wife. Me and Tameka hung with you and your wife." Jeff stared at him. "Man, we worked together on equations to solve for time travel."

Jeff laughed, "Now, I know you're crazy."

"I'm not."

"Look, I respect you because what you and your dad did is amazing. But I don't know you or this

Tameka person. I'm not married, and time travel is impossible. Take care."

Jeff walked away, leaving DJ in disbelief. Things had changed. His father was alive and that act of saving him caused his mother to die from cancer. He never met Jeff and he cannot say for sure he is Tameka's husband. "I need to call her to see if we're still together."

Before he could call, Derek Sr. cornered him. "Son, me and Connie are going to Lumpkin's. How about you and that beautiful daughter-in-law of mine join us in an hour?"

"Sounds good, dad. I'll ask her."

"Great. See you in an hour."

DJ shook hands with several people and found his way out of the building. He realized he did not know which car was his until he reached into his pocket and found the keys. DJ looked at his license to see if he lived in the same home. He did. *"Maybe Tameka is still my wife. God help me if she isn't. There I go, asking a mythical figure to help me. But is He mythical, given all I've seen? I'd better get my life right, not that I can get out of that stupid contract."*

DJ pulled the car into the driveway as he did hundreds of times. The neighborhood appeared the same. He got out and walked inside. DJ stopped at the door in surprise. Things appeared different inside the house. The furniture was different; the curtains were different, but the stain where he wasted wine last week was there. Some things were the same, while others were different. That pit in his stomach he felt when Tameka told him about Evan reemerged.

A voice rang out from the top of the stairs. "Hey, I didn't know you made it home." She ran down the stairs. "I heard the great news! You're amazing." She planted a kiss squarely on his lips, then pulled back. "What's wrong? Your dad said you were acting strange."

"I don't know exactly. I feel a little disoriented, and I'm forgetting things too."

"What? We need to get you to a doctor."

DJ stared at the woman who he realized was his wife. He met Donna Williams in college, and they worked on a project together in freshman science. She was attractive, but because of Tameka, he did not pay her much attention. He remembered telling Tameka their love would bring them together, no matter what. Now, he realized those words were hollow and life can change your path so that you never meet.

Donna said, "Let's take you to the hospital. I'll call your dad and cancel."

"No! I want to go to dinner… with my dad. I'll be fine, Donna."

"Okay, at least you remember my name. Now, how about you go upstairs and get dressed? We don't want to be late."

"I'll do that. Thank you." DJ rushed upstairs, wondering how much changed in his life. The biggest change is the woman he loved is no longer his wife. Now Donna Williams is his wife, and he has no feelings for her. "*How am I going to pull this off? This woman is my wife, yet I know nothing about her. I have to get to a computer to learn something about this world. I need to find Tameka. I'm sure our love will prevail across timelines.*" DJ got dressed and walked downstairs.

Donna said, "Now let's go." The couple left the house. Donna continued, "I'll drive, in case you're still having memory issues."

DJ nodded in agreement. He sat on the passenger side of Donna's SUV, hoping the conversation would be light. Donna asked, "I know today is a day of celebration for you, but I haven't forgotten the sadness it also brings." DJ did not know what she meant, so he nodded, hoping that would suffice.

Donna looked repeatedly at DJ. He stared out the window, praying she would not continue to talk about the meaning of the day. Donna said, "Hey look, DJ, the 24th anniversary of the loss of your mom falling on the day of your biggest success can't be easy."

DJ looked at her. His look was intense with learning that his mom had passed on this day 24 years ago. The thought of trading one parent's death for another one brought sweat to his forehead. The beads rolled down the side of his face. He struggled for air, but none was coming. He rolled down the window.

Donna asked, "What are you doing? Are you hot?"

"I just needed some air."

"I'm sorry. I shouldn't have brought it up. We should focus on the celebration."

"It's okay, Donna." They made it to the restaurant. DJ did not remember the restaurant as Lumpkin's. In his timeline, it was called Maceo's. The life of one man affected more things than he expected.

The couple walked into the restaurant. DJ spotted his father and another woman sitting in a booth. They walked to the booth and Derek Sr. stood, "Welcome you two. It's good to see you both."

Everyone embraced, and Donna and DJ took their seats. Derek Sr. asked, "Son, are you feeling better?"

"I'm getting there dad." Inside it overjoyed him to be eating dinner with the man he lost 25 years earlier in his timeline. Saving him cost him his relationship with his mother. He had memories of a woman who died 24 years earlier.

Derek Sr. continued, "I know this is a hard day for us, but we have to put that to the side and embrace our success."

Connie chimed in, "Yes, today is the biggest day of your career. Enjoy it."

Her words ate at his soul. "Excuse me, but who are you?"

Confusion rested on everyone's face. "Who am I? Are you sure you're okay?"

DJ let his guard down again. It was clear she was his new stepmother, but he did not know her. He only knew his mother, and despite losing his dad, his mom never remarried or dated. This was another twist to his traveling back in time.

Dinner went on. It was uncomfortable for DJ. The memories of those at the table did not match up with what he remembered. Major events in history changed because one man's life was spared.

DJ and Donna headed home. Now would be the time he could get on a computer and figure out what was going on. Hopefully, he could find Tameka and reunite with her in this timeline. He realized she would not remember their love, but if they were to meet again, she would fall in love with him again for sure.

Once they arrived home, Donna went upstairs to go to sleep. DJ made up an excuse to go to the basement. He did not want to make love to her. In his mind, he would be committing adultery. He thought it was odd to commit adultery with someone to whom he was married. Time travel had his mind twisted in several places.

Once on his computer, he pecked away, searching for any online footprint for Tameka. *"How could my dad be responsible for Facebook not rising to power?"* In this timeline Facebook was called iFriend, and he had an account. He did not know any of the passwords, but he guessed most of them. Once in iFriend, he searched for Tameka. *"Thank God she has an account."* He sent her a friend request, praying she would respond.

After an hour, she accepted. He sent her a private message asking if she remembered him. She replied she did and asked him how he was doing. DJ replied, asking her if she would meet him for drinks. It took her a while to answer, but she agreed to meet him at a local club.

DJ left the house. He arrived at the club and took a seat with a clear line of sight to the door. He wanted to see Tameka walk in. DJ was excited inside, but he had to remember that she did not share the same timeline as he did. The last time he saw his wife, she was sleeping in bed. If he had left time travel alone, he would be sleeping with her now.

Cherelle Burton walked past his table. DJ said, "Cherelle?"

Cherelle replied, "Do I know you?"

The realization that he was not in his timeline hit him again, "I'm sorry, I thought you were someone else."

"But you said my name. Is this someone else named Cherelle as well?"

"Yes, she is. Her name is Cherelle Burton. Her husband is a friend of mine. You two look alike."

She half smiled, "Who are you really? Did Jeff put you up to this?"

DJ was more confused. Maybe Jeff and Cherelle knew each other but never married. "I do know a Jeff from work."

"My boyfriend's name is Jeff Burton. You mistook me for someone named Cherelle Burton. If I marry Jeff, then that would be my name. Come on, he put you up to this, didn't he? Is he going to propose to me?"

"Look, I'm sorry. I shouldn't have said anything." He noticed Tameka walk in. "I have to go. Good luck with the marriage thing." He looked at Tameka and she was still a beautiful woman. Nothing about that changed. He walked up to her and said, "Tameka… wow, you look gorgeous."

"Thank you, DJ."

He led her to their booth, and they sat down. He looked into her brown eyes and fell in love again. She looked at him, expecting him to say something, but she captivated his heart so much he did not know what to say.

Tameka turned her head, emphasizing she was waiting for him. DJ shook off his desires for her, "I'm guessing you're wondering why I called you here."

"I'm running out of patience."

"I remember you from back in the day. My dad taught you the piano, but I'm not sure what happened to you."

"Well, our mothers were friends and when your mom passed… sorry for your loss… I stopped coming around. I remember you were sad about it, and you cried a lot. I felt really bad for you because Mrs. James was always nice to me."

"So, we never hung out?"

"Hung out? Dude, you were three years younger than me, so that would have been a 'no'. Not that you weren't cool and all, but we didn't hang in the same circles. After we left the church, I rarely saw you."

DJ's heart dropped. This confirmed that love doesn't travel through time. They never shared the grief of his father through their mothers. Since his father did not die, Tameka's mom did not come to the house to comfort his mom. Then, when his mom passed, he did not see her again.

"So, tell me about yourself?"

"DJ, what are you doing? I know you're married. You're all over the news with this discovery of the cancer cure. They're calling it the James Miracle. There's no detail of your life that isn't exposed. What do you want from me?"

"If I truly told you, you would think I'm crazy."

"To be honest, I'm a little weirded out right now."

DJ rationalized he had nothing to lose. "If I share this with you, will you promise not to tell anyone?"

"Okay, I guess. Wait, not even my husband?"

"Husband?" DJ was so captivated by her beauty that he never noticed the rock on her finger. Tameka was married, crushing DJ's entire world.

"Yes, husband. Didn't you look at my profile? We got married a month ago."

DJ felt that pit in his stomach. In the timeline he lived, Tameka was his first and only. He was her first and only. Now, she does not know him. "No, I didn't realize you were married. Who's the lucky man?"

"Evan Clinger. We work together. Although now he's looking for another position, so we won't have to deal with that whole thing."

"Evan, it figures. In my timeline, they were attracted to each other and now, without me, they fall in love and get married. I've truly screwed up. I need to go back and change things." DJ said, "Okay, congratulations."

"Okay, so what do you want to tell me?"

"Not sure that it matters now."

"I got out of my bed with my new husband to come meet you. I did that because our mothers were friends and I realized today is the anniversary of her death. Please don't make me angry for making that choice."

She was the same Tameka in every way. The difference is the choices that were made. He said, "In another timeline, you and I were married."

"I'm out." She stood up.

"Wait, wait… please just hear me out, no matter how ridiculous it sounds." She looked at him and retook her seat. "Look, 25 years ago, my father was murdered. Apparently, this cure for cancer started back then and someone hired a hitman to kill him. I was with my father when it happened. It imprinted on me, and I dedicated my life to science. I wanted to travel back and save my father."

Tameka's face was twisted. "I know you don't believe me, but after my father was murdered, our mothers became great friends. You were at my house every day. We were so close that we fell in love with each other and got married."

Tameka nodded her head and popped her lips. "It's true, Tameka. You begged me not to go back in time. You said that changing the past would ruin the world. I haven't seen the world ruined yet, but my world… is ruined because I don't have you in it."

"Look, DJ, you have the makings of a great sci-fi novel, but I'm not buying any of it. It was nice seeing you again."

"You love sleeping in the nude except after sex. Your favorite act is kissing. You love it because it brings a connection between people greater than any other act. You used to say, 'A good passionate kiss can take you a long way.' You're always slow when getting dress."

"Anyone who's gone anywhere with me would know that but the other things… who have you been talking to?"

"No one. I figure our paths may have changed in the timeline, but you are still the Tameka I've known all my life. Those things probably haven't changed."

"You're right, that's all me, but I can't get with that time travel stuff. All I know is the life I'm living, and I barely know you."

"I understand, Tameka. I just had to tell you."

"So, you went back in time and saved your father. I guess now, with the cure, you can go back and save your mother." DJ's eyes popped. He hadn't thought of that. Tameka continued, "But wait, that would mean they would never discover the cure because your dad wouldn't be motivated to discover it. How does that all work?"

"Time travel is complicated, but I only get one more chance to go back in time. I went back to save my dad and now my mom is gone. I can't seem to win."

"Wait, so your mom was alive in the other timeline?"

"Yes, she never had cancer and died. In fact, you were great friends with my mom. I mean, you were her daughter-in-law, and she loved you."

Tameka asked, "I hate to say this but could saving your dad have caused your mom to get cancer? I mean, could he have brought home research and infected her?"

"Who knows? All I know is everything that I had is gone, but my dad is alive. I won't tempt fate again, that's for sure."

"Okay, well, DJ, I have to go. I'm sure my husband is wondering where I am."

"Thanks for coming to meet me. Take care of yourself."

"You too, DJ. I wish you the best, and again congratulations on your discovery. Wait, is it your discovery? I'm so confused."

"It's not my discovery, but it is my discovery. I know it's crazy, but I have to live in this world I created."

She smiled, patted him on the shoulder, and walked away. DJ thought, *"I should have never done this. My heart hurts more than anyone in this timeline will know. She was my everything, but now she belongs to someone else. Why didn't I listen to my wife?"*

DJ returned home to find Donna in bed. He grinned when he realized both women had similar physical characteristics, tall, dark skinned and pretty. He wished he could love Donna like he loved Tameka.

He lay down beside her. She stirred with his movements. He tried to be still. Knowing Tameka was married to another man did not make it easier for him to be with a strange woman. The Donna Williams he knew could be nothing like the one he is married to. He had to wait to see what would happen in the coming days. DJ drifted asleep thinking of the decision to go back in time and how it ruined his life.

The next day, Donna woke DJ up from his sleep. "Hey, honey. Did you have a nightmare or something? You were calling out for your dad."

"Really? I guess I did." DJ could not remember the dream, but it was likely the same dream he had for years.

"What smells so good?"

"It's your breakfast. I made you your favorite strawberry and banana pancakes with turkey bacon and grits."

"Wow, it smells delicious. Thank you."

"You're welcome. Come on down."

DJ hurried downstairs and sat at the table. He took a sip of his coffee first. "This is the best coffee I have ever tasted."

Donna twisted her head, "It's how I always make it, honey. I know how you like it."

"Wow, you sure do. These pancakes are delicious."

Donna laughed, "Honey, you are acting as if I have never cooked for you before. You know I'm the best cook you ever had in your life."

DJ had to play it off somehow. "Yeah, you certainly are. I guess I've been so involved in the discovery of the cancer cure that I had forgotten. Forgive me for that, but my oh my, this is good!"

Donna laughed even more, "Well, it will be good having you home more."

"You know we have to be involved in the cure's distribution, so maybe not that fast." The look on her face was not what he expected. "But, hey, I will make it so I'm not that involved in the details. My work is over and I'm going to take good care of my new wife."

"New?"

"Well, it's like new, right? Now that this is over, we can start again, like new."

"Got 'cha, DJ. Can we go to Jamaica?"

"Jamaica, Cancun, Aruba… you name it, we'll go."

Donna squinted her eyes, "Honey, there is something truly wrong with you. You're not remembering things, are you?"

"Why do you ask that?"

"Cancun and all of Mexico have been off limits for three years, since that outbreak of COVID killed millions."

DJ looked up at Donna. She was worried about his memory, but she could not know that he was not from this timeline. He said, "That completely slipped my mind. Honey, don't worry, I am good. Trust me. I guess I need to get dressed and head out to work."

"Yes. I'm headed out now." She kissed DJ. This time, he tried to be the passionate kisser he was with Tameka. "Now, that's the way my man kisses me. Have a blessed day, honey."

"Thanks, you too."

"Oh, I'm going straight to church after work."

"Okay."

"Will you meet me there?"

DJ was shocked. *I go to church?* He answered, "Yes, baby, I'll meet you there. What time again?"

"Seven, honey. Bye."

"Bye." She walked out the door and DJ flopped on the couch. The changes in this timeline were many and he could not keep up. Now he had to find the church they attended and meet Donna there. He would need to spend the day trying to figure everything out. Most of all, he hoped he would see Diablo again and find out if saving his father truly costed his mother her life, a detail Diablo left out.

DJ arrived at work. He chuckled at the name of the company, never believing he would see his name on a building. Derek James Pharmaceuticals was renowned for providing top medicine at a cheaper rate. His father did not believe in charging people hundreds of dollars for their health. Instead, he wanted everyone to have a chance at affordable healthcare.

Once inside, he walked to his father's office. Derek Sr. discussed the distribution of the cure to centers around the world. Once he hung up, he greeted DJ, "My son, how are you this fine morning?"

"I'm good, dad. You're amping up distribution already."

"We need to get this out there. We can't have another Mexico on our hands."

"Mexico?"

Derek Sr. looked at his son, "Don't make me bring up that fiasco. I know I rushed to judgement with that version of the cure, but I thought it would work. I did not know that the effects would be devastating when combined with the COVID virus."

"Right, you couldn't have known." DJ played it off this time rather than look like he was having memory issues. "Dad, I'm going to do some work in my office. I'll leave you to this."

"Hey, don't be late for the press conference."

"Press conference? What time is that?"

"One o'clock, in the lobby. All the news media types will be there. We're officially launching the cure worldwide."

DJ did not like the decision. He knew his father means well, but it all seemed rushed to him. "Sure, I'll be there, dad." DJ hurried to his office where he could do some research. He looked through the company files, trying to get up to speed on what was happening. The research was impressive. *Dad is smart, but I think he's overlooking some things. This cure is like the one that caused the breakout in Mexico. I need to stop this.*

DJ shut off his computer. Two men came into his office with his secretary. She said, "I'm sorry, sir. I know you said not to bother you, but they're security."

"Sir, I'm Steve Strain, Chief of Security. Why are you searching through secured files?"

"I'm the chief assistant to my father. I have a right to see the files. Why? Is there a problem?"

"When anyone opens those files, they send an alert to us, and we have to check it out. It seems you have clearance, but we had to ensure it was actually you who accessed them."

"It was me."

"Thank you, sir." The men left the room, leaving DJ with his secretary, "Amanda, I have to talk to my father. If anyone calls, tell them I'm busy right now."

"Yes, sir."

DJ hurried down the hall to his father's office. He popped in while his dad was talking to some men. Derek Sr. said, "I'll be right with you, son. Just give me a few minutes."

"Sure, dad." DJ could tell something was off. The flustered look on his dad's face told him there must be a problem. Maybe someone discovered the same flaw in the cure he did. A few minutes went by, and the men came out. One of them stared at DJ, then continued on his way.

DJ went inside his dad's office. "Dad, what was that all about?"

"Just some questions about the disappearance of one of our scientists."

"Who disappeared?"

"Jeff Burton. He was new here, only been here a week, but they thought it may have something to do with the James Cure." Derek Sr. smiled, "How about that son, a cure named after us."

"Yeah, that's great, dad. I just talked to Jeff yesterday. He seemed fine."

Derek Sr. sighed, "Yeah, I talked to him yesterday too, but he didn't seem fine to me. He seemed flustered, like he was going through something. I don't know what it was and frankly, I don't have time to figure it out. We have a cure to launch."

"That's what I came here to discuss with you. I think there's a flaw in the cure. Actually, I think it's no different from the one that caused the outbreak in Mexico."

Derek Sr. looked at his son. "Are you seriously saying that? Have you forgotten our conversation?"

The puzzled look on his dad's face concerned DJ. "Dad, I've not been myself lately, so refresh my memory."

Derek Sr. continued to look puzzled, "Who are you? You are not my son?"

The comment worried DJ. His dad was the smartest man he knew, and he figured out DJ was not the DJ he knew. "Dad—"

"No, I'm not your dad. Who are you? Answer me before I call security."

DJ sighed, "If I answer you, I don't think you will believe me."

Derek Sr. dropped some files on his desk, then took his seat. He motioned for DJ to do the same, "Try me."

DJ eased down in the seat. "Dad, I am your son, but you… you aren't supposed to be here."

"Excuse me?"

"Twenty-five years ago, you were gunned down by a man walking down our street. You were taking me to the park when it happened. It imprinted so hard on me that all I wanted was to travel back in time and save you. I dedicated my life to science and time travel."

"Are you telling me you discovered how to time travel? That's huge!"

"No, dad. I didn't. I could never solve the equation to open the wormhole and travel through it. I mean, we detected hundreds of micro wormholes, but we could never enlarge one big enough for a human to travel through."

"Who are we?"

"My assistant and friend, Jeff Burton."

"What? The guy who's missing?"

"He doesn't know me in this timeline. Apparently, I never got a job at Radford Technology, and I never met Jeff at that science conference we attended."

"Radford Technology; what is that?"

"It's a large… I'm guessing it doesn't exist in this timeline, but Tony Radford built a corporation. His lab was one of the largest in the world. He hired many scientists."

"Radford, Radford… that name sounds familiar." Derek Sr. searched his computer. "Oh, here we go, Tony Radford, a science guru who specializes in science and the supernatural. He believes where science leaves off the supernatural begins. A quack for sure."

DJ popped his lips, "Not so much, dad."

"Really? Don't tell me you believe in this garbage."

"I do now. How do you think I did all this?" DJ read his father's face. "I met a man who told me about the supernatural and this abyss that can take me back in time. However, there are rules to it. I guess physics has rules, so why not the supernatural? Anyway, I jumped into the abyss and there I was… back in our old neighborhood a day before you were murdered." Derek Sr. frowned. "The next day I waited for the man to approach. When he did, I jumped him. We struggled, but he got away. He didn't kill you. So I thought my mission was over. It wasn't. It turns out he was hired to kill you. I tracked him down at the park you took me to, tackled him again, but this time the gun went off and killed him. I tracked down the guy who hired him, but strangely enough, he jumped off the balcony in front of me.

That ended any attempts on your life. Now you're here, but mom isn't."

"What does that mean?"

"I haven't pieced it together, but mom never had cancer in the other timeline. By saving you, I killed my mother."

"That's crazy…"

"What? Why did you pause?"

"I remember that day in the park when the gun went off and that man was dead. I didn't think it had anything to do with me. I wasn't that important, but I had this experiment going in my lab. I knew it would change lives. I remember your mom coming to the lab and she accidentally knocked over some test tubes with viruses in them. They were harmless separately, but together they clearly were deadly. I think that may have caused her cancer."

"So, if you had died, she never would have been in that lab to knock over those tubes."

"Yes, it seems that no matter what you do one of your parents won't survive."

DJ nodded his head. His father confirmed what he dreaded. The fee for saving his father was losing his mother. He traded one pain for another one. Not to mention losing his wife and good friends. This unfamiliar world was not kind to DJ. He had to fix it.

Derek Sr. said, "Why don't you go back and stop the man again, then stop your mom from coming to the lab that day. Then you'll have both of us."

"I can't, dad. If I go back again, I won't be able to return to you."

Derek Sr. smiled, "But son, you'll already be with me. The younger version of you will grow up with both parents. I can't imagine what good that would be for you. You struggled mightily with losing your mom. Then, when Connie came into the picture, you never truly forgave me."

"I could see that. I felt I wasn't too fond of her last night, and I know I was with mom after losing you. I also lost my wife because I was too focused on time travel. I guess that's my curse. When I focus on something, I really focus on it."

"It's hard to imagine you and Donna breaking up. You love each other."

"Donna wasn't my wife, Tameka was. You taught her piano when I was young."

"Wow, I hadn't thought of that little girl since your mom passed. I wonder what she's up to?"

"She's married. Another mistake with time travel."

Derek Sr. placed his hands on his desk, "Son, if you can take a trip through time, then there has to be a way to fix all of this so that you get everything you want. When you went back before, you didn't realize that these other changes would take place. Now you're armed with that knowledge. Note everything that's changed and when you go back this time, don't let those ripples happen. Keep Tameka close to you. Don't let your mom go to my lab, etc."

"I can only stay for two days, and I can't come back."

"I got to believe there's a way around that, too."

DJ stood up, "Well, now you know why my memory isn't straight on a lot of topics. But this cure, it's wrong. It's basically the same one as the one in Mexico."

"Actually, it is the same one. We made some minor adjustments in the amounts to reconcile the mutation and to fight off COVID."

"Dad, we have to make sure this will work this time. Millions died in Mexico."

"Son, this was your idea. Mexico was a mistake I made, but we fixed it this time. We can't stop now, or thousands will be out of a job. I realize you're not familiar with this company, but we are the largest lab in the world, not Radford Technologies from your timeline." DJ did not respond. He has doubts about it. Nothing like this happened in his timeline, so he had no frame of reference. Maybe this would be a good thing, but he could not stop it now. "Come on, son. Let's head to the lobby."

Father and son headed to the lobby to announce the plan to cure cancer for those infected. DJ knew that curing cancer would be a great thing and if the cure truly worked, he could take it back in time and heal his mom. However, he could never return home. It was a price he would pay.

They arrived in the lobby. It was crowded with media representatives trying to be the first to break the news. DJ was impressed with what the world wanted to know about his dad. *"If only they knew he was never supposed to be here."* DJ took a seat at the podium and watched as his dad spoke about the miracle drug, James-37. He listened, but his mind focused more on what he could do to save his mom. With only one trip through the abyss left, it would need to be a sacrifice for her and his younger self.

One reporter asked Derek Sr., "Mr. James, how does this miracle pill work exactly?"

Derek Sr. answered, "As part of its normal function, the immune system detects and destroys abnormal cells. This most likely prevents or slows down the growth of most, if not all, cancers. Let me give you an example. We sometimes find immune cells in and around tumors. These cells, called tumor-infiltrating lymphocytes or TILs, are a sign that the immune system is responding to the tumor. People whose tumors contain TILs often do better than people whose tumors don't contain them. James-37 will supplement TILs for those people who tumors don't contain TILs."

The reporter asked a follow-up question, "But what about cancer cells that avoid destruction by TILs or your miracle drug?"

"You've been doing your homework. It is true genetic changes can make cancer cells transparent to the immune system. They can have proteins on their surface that turn off immune cells or the normal cells around the tumor can interfere with the immune system and stop it from healing the patient. However, with James-37, most patients can and will beat cancer."

Another reporter asked, "You seem very sure of this, Mr. James. Have you had human trials?'

"Yes, we have, and 92.9 percent of our patients have survived. You can check the records on that. The FDA has been involved with this every step of the way. We couldn't have done it without government help. That will be all the questions. As I stated earlier, the first batch of James-37 will arrive at cancer centers around the world tonight. Tomorrow, let the healing process begin!"

DJ joined his dad as they walked away. In the elevator, DJ said, "Dad, I saw the research, and we didn't have a 92.9 percent success rate. We only tested four people and three of them displayed a decrease in cancer cells. We need more time."

Derek Sr. hit the stop button. "We don't have time, DJ. Suck it up. This drug has to work, or this company will go under! We'll have nothing left. Can't you understand that?"

"But, dad, these are people's lives. We have to be sure."

"I wish you were the old DJ. He would understand."

Derek Sr. left DJ standing in the elevator, disappointed that his father was disappointed in him. *"I've got to help save these people."*

DJ sat in his office. Amanda came in and asked him, "Would you like me to get anything for you, sir?"

"No, thank you. Hey, how about a time machine? Can you get that?"

She laughed, "No, can't help you there, sir." She walked out of the office.

DJ's phone rang. It was his private office line. "Hello."

"Is this DJ?"

"Yes, who is this and why are you altering your voice?"

"Someone is trying to kill me. I pointed out problems with the cure, problems that I believe will kill a lot of people. I noticed something different about you yesterday. Something changed. I'll meet you, but it has to be a place of my choosing."

"Name it."

"830 First Street, Northwest. The building is called UCP. I'll meet you in front of the building in an hour."

"UCP? I've never heard of it."

"That's a good thing. Come alone. I don't trust anyone and if you're not alone, then I will disappear, never to be seen again."

"I'll be there." DJ hung up the phone. Now he was into some cloak and dagger stuff. Stuff he did not need to be in. He needed to focus on saving his mom and the millions he believed would die if they take the cure.

DJ took a ride share to the meeting location. He stood outside the large building that housed CNN and the Department of Education. He did not understand why the caller chose this location, but it was fine with him.

DJ watched the people passing by, wondering which of them would need the cure and which would not. He suspected everyone would be infected in two weeks. Ironically, a cure for the cure would be necessary.

DJ recognized the large man approaching him. Jeff stood six, four, so he could not be missed in most places. DJ's heart grew happy seeing him. "Jeff, I'm glad to see you, man."

"You're very different from the DJ, I know. Why is that? What happened in the last week?"

"Here we go again."

"What does that mean?"

DJ sighed, "Look, let's skip all the details and sum it up like this. We knew each other in another timeline. I traveled back to save my dad, it changed everything and now I believe the world is in danger because of my recklessness."

"Time travel? I've always been smitten by the theory; what it would be like to travel back in time. What was it like?"

"You're the first person to accept my explanation without question. Again, to sum up time travel, somethings are better left for God."

"Understood. If you had to do it all again, would you?"

"That's the million dollar question. I lived without my dad for 25 years. Seeing him in action, I question my drive. He's not the man I knew when I was five years old. Not to mention I traded my mom's life for my dad's."

"What?"

"Saving my dad meant my mom went to his lab and contracted a virus that gave her cancer. She died the next year."

"Wow, you're right; some things are better left for God."

"What do we have here?"

"DJ, that cure won't work. I told your dad my findings, and he said that he knew there would be problems. Next thing I know, someone is taking a shot at me. I know he's your dad, but I think he's trying to cover this up."

"I know he's covering it up."

"They killed my fiancée, man. I'm going to bring them down."

"Cherelle? I just saw her the other night."

"You know Cherelle?"

"I knew both of you from the other timeline."

"Got it." Jeff handed him a USB drive. "This is all the information I gathered. Everything else is up to you."

"Thanks, Jeff, but I don't have a plan for any of this yet. I may need your help. Where can I reach you?"

"I'll contact you." Jeff hurried away, leaving DJ by himself in the middle of a crowd of employees going in and out of the building. He flagged down another ride share and retrieved his car from work and headed home.

On the drive home, DJ pondered his future. *"What am I going to do? Do I try to fix this world going forward or take my last trip into the past? Too many consequences to worry about. I need a drink."*

He drove past True Gospel Ministry and turned around. *"I need to talk to a pastor."* He pulled into the parking lot of the church and walked to the entrance. He hoped someone was there to have a conversation with.

Once inside, DJ spotted several people sitting on the pews and others kneeling at the altar. A man came up to him, "Hey, brother. Are you here for prayer?"

"No, I'm here to talk to the pastor if he has a minute."

"Hold on, he's in the middle of prayer."

DJ waited by the entrance. He watched the people in the church praying. He wondered what they would do if they faced the devil like he did. *"I wish I would have come to church more often. That's the curse of believing in science. You think you have all the answers and then one day you find out you don't. I know these people believe God is real, but they've never seen God. I've seen the devil in person and if he's real, God is definitely real."*

After some time, DJ decided to leave. The pastor was extremely busy, and it appeared he would not get to DJ anytime soon. He turned to walk out, but the man grabbed him by the arm. "Wait, brother. He'll be with you in a minute."

"I don't have any more time to wait." *"That's ironic. I for one, know we have plenty of time if you use your jumps into the abyss correctly."* DJ sighed, "I will come back tomorrow." He broke the man's grip on his arm and walked out of the church. *"See, when one seeks God, one gets denied access. How can I serve a God like that?"*

DJ got into his car and headed home. He wondered how he would deal with Donna. She would pick up on him not being the man she married. He would have to explain to her he's not from this timeline. *"How many people am I going to share this story with? Sooner or later, it will be breaking news on television and I'll once again be the laughingstock of science."*

He walked into the house. Donna and Derek Sr. were sitting on the couch. DJ recognized something was wrong. He figured his dad told Donna about the time travel story, but he did not know how he had spun it. DJ said, "What's up? Why the faces?"

Donna looked at Derek Sr. and said, "Honey, I know you've been under a lot of pressure, but we can help you."

"What? Dad, what did you tell her?"

"Son, I told her the truth. Launching this miracle cure has you so uptight that you have imagined that… well, you're not you. Come on son, time travel is impossible? You are trying to reconcile that you're not a part of this when you are. I'm the face of the company, but we all know you are the brains."

"Dad, the time travel story is the truth. You believed me in the office."

"No, I didn't. I just coddled you to help you get through the announcement. Now it's time to get you some help. I've called my friend at one of the outpatient clinics. He can help you."

"Dad, are you serious? I'm not going there."

"Yes, son, you are."

Donna said, "DJ, it's for your own good, honey. I'll come with you. It's an outpatient clinic, so after you see the doctor, you can come home."

"I'm not going." DJ turned and rushed out the door. Headed to his car he saw a van heading to the house. He spun out of the driveway and down the street. The van stopped at his house. *"My dad is trying to have me committed so my truth won't get out. I've got to get somewhere and get the word out before he tarnishes my name."*

Chapter 9

DJ drove into the city. He stopped at a store. He knew if he used his credit card, they would know his location. "Only a twenty on me, so that's going to have to due." He pumped $15 in gas into his car, then went inside to grab a drink. He noticed two men in the store and a black woman behind the counter. They all stared at him when he came inside. DJ blew it off, thinking they recognized him from television. He grabbed his drink and headed to the counter. No one moved. The lady pointed her eyes at the men.

One of them said, "Put your hands up, mister!"

DJ put his hands up. The men instructed the cashier to give them all the money. The older looking man forced DJ to put his hands on the counter. They took DJ's wallet with all his credit cards and the twenty in cash. They rushed out of the store. DJ asked the cashier, "Are you okay?"

"I'm shaken but I'm alright. I'm calling the police."

DJ waited with her until the police came. Detective Kai Jeter arrived with uniformed officers. She asked, "You two are witnesses to the crime?"

DJ answered, "Yes, I just came in to get a drink after pumping my gas. I guess the robbery was already taking place when I walked inside."

The cashier added, "Yes, that's correct. The men came in a little before DJ came in. They pulled out their guns but when he walked inside, they paused to see what he would do."

Detective Jeter said, "You two know each other?"

DJ answered, "No, why do you say that?"

"She called you by name."

"Oh, I told her my name afterwards, while we were waiting for you. Her name is Belinda. We made small talk."

"You look familiar."

DJ said, "You've seen my face all over television the last few days. I'm Dr. Derek James Jr., one of the scientists who discovered the miracle cure."

"Ah, got you Dr. James."

"DJ is fine."

Detective Jeter said, "We're going to need both of you to come down to the station and write your statements."

Belinda said, "I can't go right now. I don't have anyone to run the store."

"Ma'am, this is a crime scene. The forensic people will need time to go over the scene. We will shut your store down for a couple of days."

Belinda sighed, "There goes that Maserati I wanted."

DJ laughed. He loved a woman with a sense of humor. It helped that she was tall for a woman and had a figure DJ loved. "May I offer you a ride in my little car? It's not a Maserati, but it will get us to the station."

"Sure, that would be awesome. Especially given my other option is to walk." They laughed again. DJ enjoyed the ride down to the station. In all the troubles he endured since he returned from the past, Belinda was a pleasant surprise. She reminded him of the early years with Tameka. He wondered if they could have a relationship, but then he realized that the answer to all the world's problems revolved around him returning to the past and staying there.

They went inside the station and the officers placed them in separate rooms. DJ thought it was strange that they put him into a room that resembled an interrogation room while they placed Belinda in a waiting room. DJ asked the officer, "Why am I being put in an interrogation room?"

"Ask the detectives when they come in. I just put you where I'm told to put you."

DJ took a seat and waited for the detective to come inside. He hoped his father had not convinced the police that he was crazy, and they were detaining him. After half an hour, Detective Jeter came inside and took a seat across from DJ. She said, "Dr. James, I'm a little perplexed here. How old are you?"

"I'm 30, but what does that have to do with the robbery today?"

"The forensic techs took fingerprints from the counter where Mrs. Clayborne said one assailant placed their hands. Now we got a hit on his prints and we're taking him down as we speak, but we also got a hit on your prints."

"Why would you get a hit on my prints?"

"Well, it struck me as odd as well. It seems your prints were at the scene of a murder."

DJ laughed. "Did my dad put you up to this? It's clear I have not murdered anyone. I may forget my wallet from time-to-time, but I think I would remember killing someone."

"Dr. James, the murder I'm speaking about was 25 years ago. The man's name was DeAngelo Platt.

The investigation revealed that he was trying to kill your father. The problem we have here is… you were five. We know the man in the park was a grown man because of witness testimony. Do you want to add anything to this?"

"You got me", DJ laughingly said. "I traveled back in time and killed the man, then came back here to my time." DJ laughed more to add emphasis to his statement. DJ nodded his head, smirked then continued seriously, "It's clear your forensics team made a mistake. Either today or 25 years ago. There's no way I could have been at the scene of that murder as a grown man. Maybe my five year old self touched something in the park that day. I don't know, but it surely wasn't me."

"We certainly can't hold you on this, but there's something going on here and I plan to get to the bottom of it."

DJ grinned, "I certainly didn't kill a grown man at five years old so, I hope you get to the bottom of it too. Now if I can write my statement and leave, I would be so gracious." She slid a notepad and pen to DJ, and he wrote out his statement.

DJ stepped out of the room after writing his statement. He headed for the front exit, not wanting to spend any more time in the precinct than he needed. Belinda sat at the front, waiting for him. "Boy, what did you write… a book?"

"They were talking to me about some case 25 years ago. They thought I had something to do with it."

"Twenty-five years ago? How old are you?"

"Thirty. Yeah, they think the five year old version of me murdered someone." Belinda frown. "Hey, don't look at me that way. It was their craziness."

"I know I'm frowning at them. If they work like this, they will never find the people who robbed my store."

DJ laughed. Inside, he knew the police were on the right track, but they would never put it together. In their world, time travel was not possible, but DJ knew in the supernatural world it was. Now he had the police asking questions and his dad trying to have him committed. It was time to save himself.

DJ dropped Belinda off at home. He wanted to ask her if he could stay, but he did not want to explain anything to her. His best plan would be to stay off the grid and sleep in his car. He returned to the very park where he killed the man who had tried to murder his dad. He thought, *"You know, it always seems to come back to this park. I wonder if in the supernatural world, there is something that links this park to my life and time travel. Who knows anymore? I'll just park and grab myself some sleep."*

DJ jumped into the backseat and closed his eyes. Twenty minutes later, someone pounded on his window. It was Jeff. DJ said, "Hey man, what's up?"

"I know they're after you. I watched as they sent people to your house."

"My dad tried to have me committed. That way he could control anything I said, make me sound crazy to the world."

Jeff sighed, "Dude, those weren't medical people. Your dad was going to make you disappear."

"What? He wouldn't kill his only son."

"Look man, Derek Sr. is not the man you think you saved 25 years ago. He needs this cure to save his company and everything he's worked for. Desperation changes a man. It changed him for the worse."

DJ knew his words may be accurate, but he had a hard time believing the man he idolized would stop at nothing to save his company. DJ asked, "As you can see, I need a place to crash. Can you help me out?"

"I can. That's why I'm here. I'm parked behind you, so follow me." Jeff got in his car and DJ followed him. The home Jeff led him to was on the edge of Washington, DC, and Maryland, just inside the Maryland border. The neighborhood was quiet and uneventful. In DJ's timeline Jeff lived in an upscale neighborhood with doctors and lawyers. This place was a far cry from that one.

DJ followed Jeff inside. The inside of his home differed from the outside. Jeff had computers and equipment everywhere. Jeff said, "I've been studying this so called cure for over two years. I knew it would work for some, but most of the people will have adverse reactions and certain death. Before they die, they will become symptomatic and spread the disease to others. DJ, if we let this out, millions could die before we even realize how bad it truly is."

DJ studied Jeff's work. "In any timeline, you are a remarkable man. That's why I worked with you before."

"I can't speak to that, but this became my passion. Now what do we do? Your dad is after both of us."

DJ thought about it, but he couldn't think of anything. "Right now, Jeff, I need to sleep. I don't know how many hours I have been awake."

"Get some rest. You can take the bedroom on the left when you get to the top of the stairs."

"Thanks Jeff. I appreciate it."

"No problem."

When DJ reached the top of the stairs, he asked, "Hey, if this is your home, why can't they find you?"

"This isn't my home. It belonged to a friend of mine who passed away a few years ago. No one knows he left it to me. I use it as a place to hide away. It's not in my name or anything and I only come here at night when the neighbors don't see me. I'm very careful."

"Hmm, so I see." DJ walked into the room. It was immaculate. Jeff kept a great house even if he did not live in it. DJ flopped down on the bed. He gave his situation some thought. Could his dad be trying to kill him? Why is Donna helping him? She's supposed to be his wife, but why would she want him dead? There were so many questions and few answers. Of course, the biggest question was if he was going to go back in time and allow his dad to be killed. *"It certainly would stop this madness from happening."*

Chapter 10

DJ woke up refreshed the next morning. He headed downstairs drawn by the beautiful aroma of freshly brewed coffee. Jeff said, "Morning, DJ. Do you want some coffee?"

"Yes Lord. Coffee and I need to be reunited." He took the cup from Jeff and sipped on it. "This is so good." DJ and Jeff both looked at the television as it blared the early reports of patients receiving the cure. "How did they use it so fast?"

"Your dad has persuasive powers. He's getting them to use it, then selling his company in an hour. He will make billions, leaving the new owner to clean up the mess."

"I was wondering how he was going to get out of it once people started dying."

"I hacked into the mainframe and found evidence of a sale. It's on the USB I gave you. The sale will be official this morning, before anyone dies from the cure."

"Do you know the incubation period?"

"My guess, 24 to 48 hours. Plenty of time to make the sale."

DJ sat down and watched intently as the news continued to give praise to James Pharmaceuticals. Flashes of Derek Sr. accepting handshakes and congratulations from leaders around the world sickened DJ. The camera locked in on Donna joining Derek Sr. on the stage. Donna and Derek Sr hugged and DJ realized why she was willing to help kill him. The thought of his father sleeping with his wife sickened him even more. He dismissed the thought when Connie took the stage and hugged him as well. "Maybe I was wrong, but still, why is she willing to have me killed?"

"Is that a rhetorical question?"

"Oh, I was just thinking out loud. I can't figure out why Donna would help him."

Jeff said, "Ask her."

"If I call, she could have it traced."

"I have some burners."

"I should have known." They both laughed and Jeff handed DJ a burner phone. DJ decided to wait until Donna was away from Derek Sr.

Jeff added, "Make sure you only use that phone for one call. You don't want to give them a chance to triangulate the call."

"Got it." DJ put the phone in his pocket. "What's the plan?"

"He's already administered the cure, so we need to be prepared for the fallout. I've been working on a cure, but I'm not even close. It's tough when you don't have the actual virus yet."

"You mean people have to die."

"Unfortunately, yes."

"In the meantime, I've got to get to my dad and Donna. I need answers."

"Hey what about going back in time? Have you decided what to do?"

"I have one more trip. If I go back again, I can't return to the present.

Jeff sighed and wrinkled his eyes, "Wow, then that's a tough decision to make, my friend."

"It is… a very tough decision for anyone to make."

Jeff shook his head, "That's too much for me to handle."

DJ asked, "What are you going to do? Continue working on the cure for the defective cancer cure?"

"Yes, and watch the news to see how it's going. Like I said I don't think anything will happen for two days."

"Great, who is the buyer for the company?"

"Channel Side. They are interested in becoming the biggest pharmaceutical company in the world. The purchase of James Pharmaceuticals would make that happen. They also want to own the cure and sell it at twice the price. Those who need it won't be able to afford it."

"Sounds like big corporations plotting to get richer and no one cares about the people."

"That's it. You'd better head over to your company. Maybe you can catch the Channel Side people and inform them of the mistake they're about to make. Be careful though, you know your dad is trying to have you committed."

"Good idea. Hopefully it will work out and I can avoid being committed." DJ headed out the front door and got into his car. The drive into DC was difficult. There were cars everywhere as rush hour invaded the district. DJ summarized it had something to do with the miracle cure celebration as well. He had no cash on him, so taking the train was out. He had to be patient on the drive.

DJ eased closer to the building. He got lucky and found a parking spot within a block. Because of his father DJ did not want to park in the garage.

After parking he spotted Donna on the street. He raced towards her. "Donna… I need to talk to you."

"DJ, we have been looking everywhere for you."

"Tell me you aren't in this with him?"

"In what and with who? Your dad said you were having a nervous breakdown over the stress of creating this cure. DJ, you need some rest, honey."

"No, Donna, I don't need rest. Are you sleeping with him?"

She frowned, "How dare you say something so nasty and despicable. You know me better than that Derek James, Jr."

"I had to ask. I don't know who I can trust. You were having me committed and then I see you hugging him on television like you love each other."

"I do love him; he's your dad, DJ. I'm going to work now."

"I'm sorry. Please, I'm sorry. I need your help."

She looked at him. DJ hoped his apology would get him somewhere. "What do you want from me, DJ?"

"I need to stop this cure. It's going to kill millions."

"Your dad believes you have lost your mind. That's why he asked me to help get you committed. He also said you believe you went back in time and saved him from death. Why should I believe anything you say? You don't even believe I'm your wife."

"Donna, can we go somewhere and talk in private. I'm not comfortable on the street."

"I have to work."

"Call in?"

"Whether you believe it or not, you're still my husband, so I will do you this one favor. Where do you want to go?"

"Anywhere off the street." DJ popped over to the passenger side and Donna got behind the wheel. On the drive DJ continued, "So my dad told you about the time travel thing."

"He did; said you've lost your mind."

"I don't know if he's serious about that or if he's trying to cover things up, but I traveled back in time. In my timeline he died. I spent my life trying to time travel back to that time and save him. Finally, it turned out to be a supernatural way, which allowed me to go back in time. I won't go into those details yet. After saving my dad, I learned he was the target of a hitman. I had to stop him from filling the contract and then stop the man who hired him. I did that. When I returned, everything was different, including you. We went to college together, but I was totally into Tameka, my wife. I guess with Tameka out of the picture, I focused on you, and we married."

"I don't remember a Tameka at college."

"I met Tameka after my father's death. Her mom and my mom were good friends. We played together all the time and fell in love with each other. Since my dad didn't die, we never connected."

"Sorry, I guess."

"Donna, it doesn't mean that what you had wasn't real. It just means that my life and my memories are different. The bottom line here is I'm not crazy and my dad needs to be stopped."

"Say I believe you, where is this Tameka now?"

"Married to someone who use to hit on her in my timeline. I guess without me they had the opportunity to connect."

Donna smiled, "So, not a threat."

"No, Donna, not a threat."

"What about us? You clearly don't love me. You don't even know me."

"I'm not saying there can never be an 'us'. All I'm saying is that if I stay in this timeline, I'll need some time."

"If you stay?"

"I have one more trip through the abyss. I'm not ruling out taking another trip. My dad needs to be stopped and I might have to be that sacrificial lamb."

"Okay, we need an alternate plan."

"Yes, we do." He paused. "Thank you, Donna, for believing in me and having my back. I really thought there was something going on with you and my dad."

She half smiled, "Your dad is very manipulative but, in the end, I have to trust my husband even if he doesn't know that he's my husband."

"I can say one thing. I must be great at choosing wives. In both timelines I ended up with the best wife." His comment brought a huge smile to Donna's face. He did not believe it was the truth, but he was happy she smiled. At first, he was leery about Donna, but now he allowed himself to be swayed to trust her.

They arrived at a house that was for sale in an unfamiliar neighborhood. DJ asked, "Where are we?"

"This is a house that I'm supposed to list for rent today. However, I think I can drag the paperwork out a bit and you can stay here. No one will know you're here… we're here. I want to stay with you and help you." DJ could not believe what he was hearing, but he was glad for the help. "Inside, the place is furnished, so we're good. We might need some items to eat. I can get something and come back."

"I'm good for now. Is there a television in here?"

"Yes, a wall mounted 60 inch I believe."

They got out of the car and Donna opened the front door. DJ marveled at the home. "Wow, how much is the rent here?"

"Oh, it's $5,000 a month."

"Whoa, rich people clearly live here."

"Yeah, they are wealthy. Most people who rent this place are athletes. They stay here during the season, then go back home afterwards. This place brings in very good money."

"I bet it does." DJ grabbed the remote and turned on the television. "I need to track the news to see what's happening. My friend said the incubation period for the virus is one to two days so there may not be much to know until tomorrow."

"Got you. I'm calling my job to tell them I'm sick. I'll be right back."

"Okay." DJ flipped the channels until he found a news station. The news focused on the sale of James Pharmaceutical to Channel Side. The stock price headed through the roof as people were buying it as fast as humanly possible.

Donna walked back into the room, "So, I am sick." She coughed a couple of times then laughed. "Anything I can do, babe."

"Not right now."

"Should I call you babe? I mean, we're married but we're not married. I'm so confused."

"In this timeline we're married." DJ stood up. Part of him wanted to hug her, but another part thought about Tameka. He asked himself, *"Am I cheating? Is it cheating?"*

DJ decided to embrace her. He kissed her on the lips and their tongues dances together. For DJ, it was the first kiss from another woman, and he cursed himself for enjoying it. He let go and Donna's eyes were closed. He said, "You enjoyed that?"

"I did. We haven't kissed in a month."

"A month?"

"You… the other version of you… whatever. You were so engulfed in your work with the cure that you didn't have time for me. I became very lonely."

Her words rang out in DJ's spirit. He heard them before, but from Tameka. It seemed no matter what timeline he lived in, he always threw himself into his work to the detriment of his marriage. DJ said, "What's his name?"

She looked into DJ's eyes, "Marlon, and it was only one time. The last month you drifted away totally but before that you rarely came around. It wore on my spirit and when you totally stopped paying me any attention, well, I went to Marlon, and he did."

The sadness in her voice cut like a knife to DJ. He knew it was not him who caused Donna to run to another man, but it did not make him hurt any less. He hugged her again. "If I stay in this timeline, you won't be lonely again."

She smiled, "Why DJ, are you smitten by me?"

"I guess I am."

"What about Tameka?"

"She's married, so there's no chance there."

Donna said, "Yes, I remember you said that, but that doesn't mean you don't have feelings for her. You were married for how long?"

"Since we were 18, so 12 years, but we knew each other since I was five, 25 years. She was, is, my world."

"Well, hopefully I will become your world."

DJ smiled hoping it made her feel good inside. "Can we get some food now?"

"Oh, of course we can, honey."

"Thanks, I'm starving. Some coffee too."

Donna smiled, "You may be in the wrong timeline but there are things about you that are the same. I think you would love coffee anywhere."

"Thank you." Donna walked out the door headed to the store while DJ continued to focus on the report of the sale of his dad's company.

DJ dosed off. He dreamed of being at a bar having drinks. He recognized it as his original timeline. After drinking, DJ paid the tab, said goodbye to Trina and walked out of the bar to his car. He got inside, questioning his ability to drive. He pulled out into the street and headed home.

In his dream, his phone rang, and it was Tameka she began nagging him about his work and time travel. He grew impatient with her and yelled at her. She hung up on him and he threw his phone. The next moment, something slammed into him.

"DJ, wake up honey!" DJ woke up, startled. "Are you okay? You must have been dreaming."

"I was. Wow, it seemed so real, but I'm glad it wasn't. Is the food ready?"

"Yes, babe, it is. I stopped and picked up some pancakes and your favorite turkey sausage. Here's your coffee, the 27 ounce Dunkin' Donuts."

"You're an angel."

"I try. Anything on the news?"

"No, the sale of my dad's company went through. He's richer than ever."

"Wow, I guess now he has no reason to commit you."

"Nope, but brace yourself. This is far from over."

Donna sat down next to him with breakfast for both of them. "I believe you. We just have to be ready."

"Breakfast for dinner, my favorite. I need to find Jeff and see how it's going with the cure. This is so good."

"It's from this little shopping center down the street. They make a great breakfast."

Jeff called on DJ's burner. DJ said, "Hello?"

Jeff answered, "DJ, you need to get here fast."

"Hey, Jeff. I was just talking to Donna about you. What's up?"

"Donna? Can you trust her?"

"Yeah, I can."

"It's starting. There are some cases in Africa and the Pacific. They're keeping it low key to not alarm anyone."

"Okay, we're headed your way." DJ jumped up, finished his coffee and said, "We have to go. I guess one to two days incubation wasn't accurate. Cases are popping up already."

"Okay, I'm ready. You drive."

"Thanks." They headed out the door. Thankfully, DJ's memory was excellent, and it did not take him long to find Jeff's hideout. They went inside and Jeff was frustrated. DJ said, "Man, are you okay?"

Jeff flung his equipment to the floor. "It's impossible. Dude, people are going to die, and my models say this thing will be out of control by the end of the week."

Donna clutched DJ's arm. Fear was etched on her face. DJ said, "Jeff, man, we can still fight this. Let me help with the calculations."

"You don't get it. It's spreading already. People who have been treated are spreading it to those who haven't been treated. It can be a touch, someone breathing on you, a kiss, whatever, this thing will spread."

One of Jeff's phones rang. He answered the call while DJ pondered his fate. He needed to fight this and fight it now. Jeff was building up a worst case scenario, but DJ believe they could stop the spread of it.

Jeff grabbed DJ by the shoulders, "You have to go back and fix this man. You have to!"

"Jeff, man, it's not that easy. First, I don't even know where the abyss is. I have to meet up with Diablo, and he has to show me."

Jeff's face twisted, "Diablo? The devil?"

"Hey, that's what he calls himself. I'm sure he's not the devil."

Donna chimed in, "My husband isn't jumping back into some abyss. What if that makes the world even worse?"

Jeff replied, "Worse than this? Do you see my numbers?"

Donna continued, "I don't need guesses. I need absolute numbers that would justify my husband going back in time again. This time, he won't be able to return."

"She's right, Jeff. If I find the abyss and jump in, I won't be able to return. It's a one way trip and imagine the damage I could end up doing."

Jeff's anger grew. "You caused this! If you hadn't gone back in time, people wouldn't be dying! Was it worth it?" He stormed out of the room.

In DJ's mind, he knew it was the truth. If he left fate alone, innocent people would not have suffered the consequences. He wanted to go back to the abyss and make it right, but he did not know how to get in touch with Diablo. DJ looked at Donna, "I know you're happy with me and the life we've built—"

"No, you're not doing this because some whacked out scientist believes it's your fault. This could have happened in your timeline too, just later."

She was right. It could be happening right now in the timeline he left. Going back may not make it right, but he had to try. "I get why you don't want me to go back, but my spirit is telling me to go."

"Your spirit? The DJ I know left church a long time ago, and he doesn't believe in God at all."

DJ snickered, "This DJ went into the abyss and when I tell you, God is real; God is real, but so is the devil. I have one trip left through the abyss, and I need to make this right. I need to find Diablo and get back to it."

"I will not let you do this. There has to be another way."

"Why are you so interested in me? What if your life in my timeline is better?"

"What was my life like?"

DJ answered, "I really don't know."

"But DJ, I know the version of you standing before me is the best of both timelines. I don't want to lose you."

DJ heard this before. Tameka said something similar, hoping to stop him from building the time machine. Both women did not want him to take the trip back in time. *"Maybe I need to listen this time."*

Donna stepped toward him and slid into his arms. "Let's find another way, baby. I know you sense what I sense. We belong together. I know you love Tameka, but I feel like your feelings are growing for me."

She was right. He felt something inside for her and maybe if he lived the life the DJ from this timeline lived, he would feel it more. Without knowing Tameka, he could love her. "I'm willing to find another solution, but I think the only one is for me to go back."

Donna asked, "What's the rush?"

"The rush? Baby, people are dying."

Donna smiled. "That's the first time you've called me 'baby'."

DJ realized it was the first time. He wondered if inside he was converting to the present timeline. He needed to talk to Diablo. "I guess it is."

"Anyway, what's the difference between going back in time today or a year from now?"

She had a great point. In time travel, it makes no difference if you go back now or a year from now. "You're as intelligent a woman as anyone I know. You're right, I don't have to rush. Let's see if there's something else we can do."

Donna hugged him, and they kissed. DJ loved the feel of her lips against his. The more time they spent together, the more he fell for Donna. DJ continued, "For now, let's get back to the house and relax. There's not much we can do without a cure and it's looking like Jeff isn't willing to work on it."

"We need to get to know each other, anyway."

The comment caused a rise in DJ's emotions. He did not have experience with a woman other than Tameka. He did not know how he would respond, but he felt something for this woman.

They walked out of Jeff's house and headed back to their home. On the ride, DJ said, "I've been so caught up on the changes in this timeline and what's going on with the cure that I never realized the change going on with me."

"Meaning?"

"I can feel my emotions and feelings changing more to you than Tameka. My initial arrival was all around me from my timeline. Now I think I'm changing. I don't remember my mother as much as I did."

"Wow, the longer you stay here, the more you change to the DJ I know."

"That's what it feels like inside. My memories of my mother, my wife, and our lives were strong. Now, I feel like I'm struggling to hold on to them."

Donna did not respond. DJ believed she did not want him to remember Tameka. The more he fell in love with her, the better she felt. They arrived at the house and went inside. DJ popped on the television and more reports of the new virus were coming across every network. Jeff's prediction model was accurate the virus was spreading and people were dying.

He looked at Donna, "There's nothing we can do. It's spreading rapidly."

"We need to get more food and supplies."

"Imagine what the stores are like right now, Donna. It will be a madhouse."

"What I got this morning will last us a few weeks, but we need a plan."

"I need to see my dad."

Donna replied, "In the morning, we'll go to his house."

"Okay." He focused on the television. The news reported the incubation time was four hours until symptoms and 12 hours until death. They believed it started with the cure; same as in Mexico, but this strain of the virus was stronger, more resistant to any medicines.

DJ felt Donna's hand caressing his hand. She slowly moved her hand up to his shoulder, then kissed him on the cheek. "Come on, honey, let's go upstairs and forget about all of this for a few hours. Tomorrow we'll be stronger."

Chapter 11

DJ woke up suddenly. He looked next to him, and Donna slept silently. He looked under the cover and realized he was naked and so was she. The dream brought back memories of a past life. He got out of bed and went into the bathroom. DJ stared into the mirror, watching the beads of sweat race down his body. He shook his head, wondering why this dream continued to plague him. She asked, "What's wrong, honey? I know I took care of my wifely duties, so it can't be that."

"I don't know. Each time I close my eyes, I have this nightmare of crashing into something in my car. I used to have a dream of seeing death all around me. All of my life I've never dreamed like this, but now these dreams are so intense and real."

"Come on back to bed, baby. You're probably letting the world's problems become yours."

"Maybe, but I can't sleep any longer."

"Who said anything about sleep?" She smiled and took his hand. Donna was very seductive, and any man would fall for her tactics. DJ realized in another life she would have a powerful hold over him, but with the memories of another wife coming and going, the struggle made him second guess any emotions he might have for her or Tameka.

The couple got into bed and began making love. DJ wanted to resist, but she was very tempting, and his resistance could not withstand her tenacity.

Before long, night gave way to day and the smell of bacon frying woke DJ from his sleep. *"It's nice to wake up to the smell of something good cooking than in a cold sweat."* He dressed and ran downstairs. Donna stood in front of the stove. When she noticed him, she smiled, hugged him, and gave him a kiss. DJ said, "You're not wearing any pants."

"You're very perceptive, Mr. James."

"I got a feeling I enjoyed watching you cook without pants."

"You would be right. You loved it and if I wasn't careful, something would jump off in the kitchen from time-to-time too."

"Is that right? Maybe we'll have to get into that again." She smiled and DJ enjoyed this moment of back and forth, but he heard a voice in his head and a stunned looked prevailed on his face.

Donna asked, "What's that look for?"

"I thought I heard someone call my name. You didn't hear that?"

"No, sir. Don't start going crazy on me, Mr. James."

"Oh, I wouldn't dare."

They sat down to breakfast. DJ's mind focused on how to fight the breakout that was happening around the world. James Pharmaceuticals was no more, but maybe the labs were still available. He said, "I know my dad sold the company but I'm going to the lab and see if I can work in there. We've got to find a way to beat this."

"Okay, how about I call your dad and see if that's possible?"

"Sounds good. See if he's still trying to have me committed. He shouldn't since he got his way now."

"I will, baby."

DJ listened while Donna talked on the phone. He wondered how much of his mind could handle the back and forth emotions of loving two women across two timelines. It was too much for his scientific mind to process. He thought about Jeff and hoped he was okay. Donna's sadness weighed on her face as she hung up the phone. She said, "We need to get to Washington Memorial."

"Why, what's going on?"

"Your dad has the virus."

"What?"

"Yes. Let's go, DJ."

The couple got up and rushed to Washington Memorial Hospital. DJ pondered the last few days, asking himself over and over how his dad could have contracted the virus. He was sure the lab used the best measures to protect those who handled the virus. He also wondered if he or Donna had it now.

They pulled into the parking garage of the hospital and headed inside. The hospital staff stopped them at the door, "You can't come inside without a mask."

DJ asked, "We don't have masks."

The staff member handed each of them a sealed mask. DJ opened it and placed it on his face. Donna did the same. The staff member said, "They probably won't help much, but they can't hurt. Who are you here to see, and you have to be an immediate family?"

"I'm here to see my dad, and this is my wife."

"Hey, aren't you the one responsible for all this?"

"No, this virus is not from the cure."

"Sure it is. Your dad is on the fifth floor. From what I heard, he's in bad shape. Not that it pains me."

DJ was furious. "What do you mean?"

Donna grabbed his arm, "DJ, don't. People are going to feel this way. Let's just go see him."

The staff member said, "Yeah, I hope you get it." He grinned as DJ and Donna walked away.

They headed to the fifth floor and asked the nurse which room Derek Sr. was in. When DJ walked inside, he gasped, "Dad? What happened?"

The nurse said, "He's delirious. It comes in the last stage. He's been mumbling all night about time travel. Asking me to tell his son to go back and fix this. Are you, his son?"

DJ hesitated, knowing what the staff member at the door thought of him. "Yes… I am."

"Does he really believe you can go back in time?"

"Like you said, he's delirious." Tears welled up in DJ's eyes. He traveled time and space, signed his life over to Diablo, only to watch his dad die a second death. Donna stood near him and caressed him.

She said, "Baby, we can beat this."

"How? My dad is dying now."

Derek Sr. jumped up. He tore the nurse's protective suit. She screamed and rushed out of the room, fearful of infection. DJ asked, "Dad, what is it?"

"You've got to save this world, son. Only you can do it. Go to the lab and fix this!" He flopped back on the bed. His body convulsed. The vitals machine beeped as doctors, nurses and technicians rushed to his side.

DJ watched as they worked on his dad. He would be the only person to watch his father die a second time. He felt the comfort of Donna's arm around him, but it would not be enough. The beeps stopped. DJ listened as the last of his dad's air left his lungs. He was dead. The doctor pronounced his death and said his condolences to DJ and Donna.

DJ froze. He appreciated the staff and Donna, allowing him to stare at his father's lifeless body. The doctor said, "Mr. James, I know this is hard for you, especially at a time like this, but you should know that we can't bury these bodies."

DJ looked at him with a cold stare. He knew where he was going with his remark, but DJ did not want to hear it. The doctor continued, "We burn them because of the virus. I hope you understand."

DJ did not respond. He kept his mouth shut because he was afraid of what he would say to the doctor. Donna answered, "He understands, doctor. Thank you."

After a few moments, DJ and Donna left the room. DJ watched the people who were dying or dead. They were in the hallways, lobbies and rooms. The hospital was overrun with death. DJ stopped dead in his tracks. He looked at the man lying dead on a gurney. Donna asked, "Did you know him?"

"I did, in the other timeline." He paused. "He's Tameka's husband in this timeline."

"Oh, my. I'm sorry."

"It's funny. I'm sorry he lost his life, but a part of me isn't sad." Donna did not reply. He knew she did not want to hear more. He tried to suppress his love for Tameka, but it kept fighting back to the top.

They left the hospital and headed to the lab. There was heavy security around the facility. Protestors in masks held signs and shouted obscenities at the lab. DJ said, "How in the world are we going to get in there?"

"Go through the garage."

"If they let us in there." DJ drove the car toward the garage, easing through the crowded streets. He pulled the car to the entrance, and the guard stopped him.

"Mr. James, you don't work here anymore."

"No, but I need access to the lab. I can help stop the spread of this virus."

The guard appeared to think about it, then he opened the gate. "Good luck, sir. We need it."

"Thanks." DJ pulled the car into the garage. They got out and went into the building. He met with more security guard resistance.

"Sir, you're not authorized to come in here."

The guard received a call. He nodded his head, then let DJ and Donna inside. DJ raced to the elevator, then to the lab area. There were scientists working desperately in suits trying to solve the issue. DJ was met by Al Coleman, owner of Channel Side. "DJ, thank God you're here."

"I wouldn't."

Al's face twisted. "Anyway, we could use your help. Tell me what you need to get started."

"Just my old station."

"You got it. We haven't touched anything yet. As you know, shortly after the sale, this virus broke out. Most think the cure triggered it. I really hope that's not the case. I spent half a billion for this company."

"I don't think that's the case. My father died over this cure."

"I'm sorry for your loss. Who is this?"

"This is my wife. She's here… well, because I don't want her to get infected."

Al said, "Great. Ma'am, we have a breakroom if you need anything to drink."

"Thank you, but I'm okay."

"Great. DJ, I'll leave you alone. If you need anything, please let me know."

"I will."

DJ sat at his computer in the lab area for hours. Donna fell asleep on the nearby couch. From time to time, DJ noticed her as she slept. She was beautiful, and he wondered how lucky he was to have two wonderful women, one in each timeline. Her sleeping distracted him somewhat, but he refocused and continued to work.

Others in the lab had minor breakthroughs, but no one was successful. DJ received a text message from Jeff. He was on to something. While reading the message, DJ heard a vile break. He turned and one scientists passed out on the floor. Others were backing away from him.

DJ woke Donna and rushed her out of the room. He said, "I don't want to take a chance of you getting infected."

"What happened?"

"I don't know, but if the virus is loose in there, we all could be infected now."

DJ watched outside the lab as they drew blood from the fallen scientist. Another scientist walked up to him, "DJ, it's good to see you." DJ did not recognize the man, but he nodded. "Vic was protected all the time. I don't know how he could have contracted the disease."

"Maybe at home?"

"He lives alone. His wife left him a year ago. They have no kids." DJ did not respond. "The only way he could have contracted it was here."

"Which means we're all infected."

"Maybe." The scientist walked away.

Donna deeply sighed. "This can't be happening."

DJ pulled Donna to the side, "I can stop all of this from happening."

"But, honey, that means you won't be with me. You'll be with her."

"But what if your life is much better? We're all going to die at this rate. I can't stand by and watch so many die knowing I can stop it. It's what my dad meant when he was dying."

Her eyes were blood red and DJ's heart ached, but he knew deep inside he had to save the world. He had to go back in time and set things back to the way they once were. Donna asked, "What happens when you go back, and you and the 5 year old you meet up?"

"I can only stay there for 48 hours. After that, I will cease to exist."

"That means the 5 year old you can grow up and start this all over again."

The comment rose a brow on DJ. He never thought of this at all happening. If he set things right, the younger version of him would be just as passionate about discovering time travel and start the events all over again. "There has to be another solution to stop the cycle of events."

Donna asked, "How do we know this hasn't happened a thousand times already?"

"We don't. I've got to figure a way to stop it for good."

Donna said, "The only way is for you to convince your 5 year old self to forget about time travel. From what I know about you, I'm sure that's right up there with parting the Red Sea."

"In this time of turmoil, I see you still got jokes." They each laughed. DJ felt good to laugh about the situation. Death was all around them, but they found something to smile about.

The scientist returned to DJ, "It's official, Vic has the virus. They are calling us all in one by one to get tested. I'm next."

DJ replied, "Good luck man. I'm sorry I don't remember your name."

"Aaron."

"Good luck Aaron."

"Thanks, DJ." He smiled at Donna and walked inside to be tested.

DJ stayed with Donna by his side. Al joined them. He said, "DJ, I want you to be tested next, then your wife."

"Okay. Have you been tested?"

"Yes, I'm negative."

DJ said, "Then you shouldn't be standing near us. We may be infected."

Al replied, "You're right." He walked away, leaving them alone in the hallway.

DJ watched as Aaron received his results. It was positive. He could tell by the look on Aaron's face it was not good news. The scientist motioned for DJ to go in next. He looked at Donna, "You first baby."

She hesitated, but then went on inside. DJ watched, hoping she would be negative. When the results returned, she cried out and went to one knee. It was positive. DJ dropped his head. He hurt inside as much as she did. He thought, *"Now she will be fine with me returning to the past to set things right. I guess that's a good thing."*

ACTIONS HAVE CONSEQUENCES

The staff led Donna to another part of the lab where positive results were being held. DJ walked inside. The testing felt like a death walk. His blood curled inside and sweat formed on his brow. He asked the scientist, "How accurate is the test?"

"It's around 97 percent accurate, sir. There have been a few false positives, but not enough to throw the test." DJ braced himself for the test. He squinched when the blood was drawn. The scientist said, "Don't like needles?"

"Never have."

"It will take a couple of minutes for the results."

"How long does my wife have to wait?"

"She can't leave. We can't allow positive people into the population. We can't control this thing as it is. If we let them leave, the virus will continue to spread exponentially."

"I understand. I just want to be with her."

"Well, we're about to see if you can or not."

"Why are you endangering yourself? Are you positive too?"

"I seem to be immune to the virus. We believe some people have a higher T-cell count which provides protection against the virus. I've been exposed equally as much as anyone else in this room and yet I'm not positive." The man paused, "Look at you. I think you're like me."

"What? I don't have it?"

"No, and by all rights, you should. Not to pry in your business, but I'm assuming you slept in the bed with your wife; you should definitely have it."

"She could have got it in the hospital when I visited my dad."

"No, according to her results, she's had it for 24 hours."

"I don't understand. I thought you should see symptoms at four hours, then death at 12 hours."

"That was the early reports. Now that the numbers have stabilized, it's more like you can show symptoms anytime between 4 and 24 hours. Death can take two to three days."

"My wife has two days to live?"

"At least you can go see her. I tested your T-cell count. You're higher than me. It's like you don't belong here or something. You can't contract the virus."

DJ looked at the scientist. He did not belong in this timeline, and it seems that is the reason he is protected from the virus. He watched his dad die for the second time. Now he has to watch Donna die as well. He knew he needed to stop all of this from happening.

Chapter 12

DJ joined Donna in the segregated space assigned to positive results. Tears were streaming down her face. She said, "No, not you too?"

"No, baby. I seem to be immune to the virus." He watched the look on her face. He could not tell if she was happy, he was immune or sad he would have to watch her die. "I have two days to find a cure for you. I will do everything in my power to find it, Donna. I promise you."

She held him, "Don't go back in time again. I know you'll find the solution to all of this. I realize you had to watch many die, but going back could make this even worse. You just don't know every variable that could happen. DJ, you're not God, and some things are meant only for God."

Her words rang out in his spirit. Again, someone told him it was not a good thing to tamper with fate. He hugged her and said, "I have to go find Jeff. I think his research is miles ahead of anything we've done here. I'm coming back for you, sweetheart. I won't let you go through this alone."

"Thank you, baby. I'm comforted knowing you're trying to find a cure. If you come back here for me, you may be distracted from finding that cure. Find it and save as many people as possible, even if that means I'm not one of those people."

"I can't do that. I came to this timeline not knowing anything about you, but somehow these emotions are in me. I love you… I can't let you die! I can't do it!"

She hugged him tighter, "DJ, go save the world. I love you too." She cried. Donna eased her way out of his arms. "Go, honey. We're all waiting for you to cure us." She walked away to another area out of DJ's sight. He dropped his head and walked out of the lab.

DJ jumped in his car and sped back to Jeff's hideout. The streets were empty of people, but cars were abandoned. He had to steer his way through them all to get out of the district and to Jeff's place. It took DJ an hour to navigate the 20-minute drive to Jeff's place. He hopped out and rushed into the house. Just as he suspected, Jeff was at his station, but his head was on the table. DJ suspected the worse.

DJ nudged Jeff, and he jumped. DJ grabbed his heart. "Man, you scared me. I thought you were dead."

"Not yet anyway. I hear they have a test, but I'm not going anywhere to take it. I don't want to risk infection. You touched me?" Jeff ran to the bathroom.

DJ shouted, "Jeff, I'm immune. I don't have it."

Jeff popped out of the bathroom, "You don't have it? How are you immune?"

"Something about a high T-cell count. Mine was the highest recorded."

Jeff snapped his fingers, "I bet it's because you traversed time and space. Your body probably compensated for the intensity of the travel through the wormhole by increasing the number of T-cells needed to fight out bacteria. You travelled twice, so your count jumped dramatically."

"That sounds logical, but we have no way of proving it."

"No need. You're immune and that's what matters. I need your blood."

"What?"

"If I can create something using your blood, maybe we can beat this thing."

"Jeff, the one way to beat it is to stop it from ever happening. All the people, including my mom, can be saved if I go back in time."

"That would mean you would have to allow your dad to die."

"That's exactly what it means."

"Can you do that?"

"I watched him die again today, at the hospital. I gained nothing by going back in time to save him. All I did was kill my mom and watch my dad destroy the world because he was too focused on saving it. My mom died of cancer, so my dad wanted badly to devise a cure for it. In the end, he's killed millions, including himself." DJ gathered his thoughts, "How close are you to a cure?"

"DJ, I feel like it's right on the tip of my brain but a thousand miles away at the same time. Your blood might have the answers, though."

DJ held out his arm, "Take some and see what you can work out. Meanwhile, I'm going to find Diablo."

"The devil?" DJ rolled his eyes at Jeff. "Okay I'm just joking man."

DJ walked outside and looked around. "I know you're here. What I don't understand is why you're hiding now." DJ drove to where he believed Lago de Fuego, the restaurant where he met Diablo, was located. He pulled up to the shopping center. The store windows were busted out and doors were kicked in. *"No one has been here in years."* The sign for Lago de Fuego hung on one nail. DJ watched the wind blow it back and forth. *"Wow, I guess even small things like this shopping center changed because I saved my dad."* He walked into Lago de Fuego and the room changed. A wave rolled across the restaurant, changing the décor from the raggedy torn down look to an immaculate establishment that looked only a few days old.

A woman stood in front of DJ. She said, "Will you be dining alone, sir?"

DJ was amazed and scared at the same time. He mumbled, "How can this be?"

She replied, "How can what be, sir?"

"Nothing… yes, I will be dining alone."

She guided DJ to the same table he sat at before. "Can I get you something to drink?"

"How about a Coke?"

"Sure."

"I'll also have my usual, the chipotle chicken, avocado melt with fries."

"Coming right up."

The hostess scurried away to get DJ's order. He wondered how long it would take for Diablo to show himself. He knew Diablo could not resist the temptation of rubbing salt into his wounds. This was what he wanted; now everyone he loved was dead or dying.

The hostess returned with DJ's order. She sat it down in front of him. It looked delicious to him; better than the first time he had this sandwich. Before he could take a bite, Diablo appeared. "Good evening, my friend. It's good to see you again."

"I was wondering how long it would take you to show up and rub it in."

"Rub it in? No, I would never do that," Diablo said laughingly.

"I need to go back again, but I don't want to stay there. I need to fix the problem I caused. Too many people are dead or dying."

"Let's not forget the lovely Tameka, too."

DJ paused. He put on a cold stare at the man everyone told him was the devil. Now, he was talking about the woman he loved first. "What did you do to her?"

"I did nothing, my friend. You changed time. I only facilitated your efforts to discover time travel."

"I want to go back."

"You can go back, but you must stay there. After 48 hours, you will disintegrate. You can't exist in the same timeline with yourself for any longer."

"I have to make another trip back to stop myself from doing all this again. My five year old self can't do it."

"I already have your soul. What else could you possibly offer me?"

"I don't have anything else."

Diablo smiled, "That's right, you don't. That is, unless you are able to convince someone else to give me their soul."

"I can't ask someone to do that."

Diablo continued to smile, "Shame, but if you love Tameka as you say you do, then maybe you should convince her to join you. If I had both of your souls, you would be together forever."

DJ thought about it, but in his heart, he could not do that to Tameka. With Donna's impending death, she would be the only one remaining that he truly loved. "I can't do that."

"Too bad. I guess there is no reason for us to talk any longer."

"Wait, wait… I'll take my one trip."

Diablo reared his head back, "That means you would die in two days."

"I understand the punishment."

"Your contract gives you the right to take that one trip. Go for it."

"Wait, you have to take me to the abyss."

Diablo laughed heartedly, "Your contract does not require that I take you to the abyss." He laughed harder, "I guess you will have to find it on your own."

"That's not fair. I need to fix this world. Don't you want me to set things back to the way they were?"

Diablo stopped in his tracks. He walked back to DJ, "Why would I want that? Because of you, I have millions of souls I would never have in the other timeline. You have sent more souls to Hell than anyone in the history of mankind." Diablo let out a hideous cry that sent curls up DJ's spine. Diablo walked away. With every step, the condition of the restaurant returned to its previous state.

DJ looked at his sandwich. He jumped at the sight of maggots coming out of it. *"Thank God I didn't eat that."* He rushed out of the abandoned building and back to his car.

DJ noticed a car sitting in the middle of the street. The driver slumped over the wheel. He went over to help the person.

He moved over to the car's driver side window. The window rolled down and DJ asked, "Miss, are you okay?"

She rolled her head and mumbled something. DJ could not hear what she said. He asked, "Ma'am, what did you say?" He put his hand on her shoulder and moved her back from the steering wheel. DJ stepped back in shock. "Tameka!" Her face was covered in sores and her eyes were blood red. "Oh, my God, what have I done?"

DJ looked in the back seat of the car. Angela was across the seat. She was already dead. "I can't stay here." He opened the door to the car and kneeled next to Tameka.

Tameka looked at him, "I know you. You're the guy that did all this to us."

"I'm sorry, baby. I only wanted to save my dad."

"But you killed us all." With her last breath, she told him he was responsible for all of their deaths.

DJ stood to his feet. He turned to head back to his car, but Diablo was behind him. He snickered, "I guess you can't convince her to give me her soul. What a shame. There's always Jeff."

"I'm not condemning anyone to my fate. I made a foolish choice and I'm paying the price."

"How about his soul for the way to the abyss?"

"No, I'd rather see this world destroyed. Hey, but how about this? I tell the world to worship God. Then you would get far fewer souls."

Diablo laughed, "Why should they believe you now? You told them the cure would save everyone from cancer."

DJ dropped his head, "You're right. They wouldn't believe me. I wouldn't believe me."

Diablo put his arm around DJ. "Give it up, son. Because of you, this world is mine. You are a part of the greatest army this world has ever known. Without your input, we would not exist."

"I want to go back and fix all of this."

"I'm sorry, my friend. I will not help you."

"You said I get three trips."

"But I did not say I would take you back to the abyss. You can have your third trip if you find the abyss. Bye - bye!" Diablo walked away laughing his hideous laugh with every step.

DJ looked at Tameka's slumped over body. He heard her words clearly in his mind, telling him not to go back in time to save his dad. It angered him she said those words because he believed she did not want his father back. The truth was, she knew the horror of changing God's grand plan. DJ got into his car and drove to the church. He prayed someone would be there to help him with his supernatural dilemma. Maybe someone could give him directions to the abyss. Diablo would not take him there because he enjoyed the state of the world. Death everywhere was what the devil wanted and because of DJ, he got it.

DJ pulled up to the parking lot where True Gospel was located. There were people milling about inside and outside the church. He deduced they were getting food and supplies. Most were probably infected or had family members who were infected.

DJ tried to hide his face. He did not want to draw attention to himself. Many blamed him, but if they only knew how much of the blame he shouldered, they would kill him a thousand times.

DJ successfully made his way inside the church. He saw the man who talked to him before. "Hey, you're that guy that was here the other day. Why did you leave?"

"I thought God was too busy for me."

"Dude, God is never too busy for any of us. The pastor might have been too busy, but God is never too busy."

DJ admired his faith in God. He wished he had the same faith, but his lack thereof put him in this situation. He asked, "Is the pastor available now?"

"He sure is. Let me get him for you."

DJ waited while the man got the pastor. In the back corner of the church, DJ recognized Gabriel, whom he met in the previous timeline. He wanted to go talk to him, but he realized Gabriel wouldn't know him. *"He doesn't look a day older than he did back then."*

The man DJ spoke with guided the pastor to him. The man said, "I don't know your name."

DJ replied, "Derek, but everyone calls me DJ."

"Well DJ, this is Pastor Howard. He's the pastor over our flock here at True Gospel."

Pastor Howard extended his hand, "Welcome brother DJ. It's a pleasure to meet you."

DJ hesitated to shake his hand for fear of the virus. Despite not being able to contract the virus, DJ could still pass the virus on to others. Pastor Howard said, "No fear, brother, I'm immune."

DJ nodded, "You too?"

"Yes, that's what the test told me. Not many of us have a T-cell count high enough to make us immune, but those of us who do are doing everything for those who don't. Especially, saving their soul."

Inside, DJ laughed. His soul was already gone and could not be saved. DJ said, "I wish that were possible for me."

"It's possible for everyone, brother."

DJ did not want to argue with the man. Pastor Howard believed in God and had faith, but DJ lived the supernatural and signed a contract that doomed him. "Okay, sir. Can I have a few moments of your time?"

"You sure can. Let's go to my office." Pastor Howard guided DJ to his office and offered him a seat. DJ sat down and admired the many plaques and awards that adorned the walls and bookshelves. He also noted there were several bookcases filled with books.

DJ asked, "Have you read all these?"

"Each one of them. Richard Steele said, 'Reading is to the mind what exercise is to the body.' I make sure I exercise my mind each day."

"I love that quote. My professor in college used to say it at the beginning of each semester to encourage everyone to read more."

"Then he was a great man. What can I do for you, DJ?"

"You likely won't believe me, sir."

"Son, I've been in this line of work for years. I was called to be a minister when I was very young. I've seen and heard many things, things people thought I never heard before. You are not the first to say that, nor will you be the last."

DJ took a deep breath, "I'm from another timeline. A timeline where none of this happens. My father was murdered when I was five. I grew up learning everything about science that I could. In the end, it was the supernatural that opened the door to me traveling back. I saved my dad, but now I've caused millions to die."

Pastor Howard looked at DJ, then let out a breath. "You were right. I have never heard this one before."

"No one has. You read about the supernatural and the powers of God and Satan. I have witnessed its power, tampered with God's plan, and now I have set the world on fire."

Pastor Howard adjusted himself at his desk, "Son, I don't believe anyone can change God's plan. What I believe here is that you are suffering from a breakdown. This virus has got all of us in an uproar and this is your way of handling it."

"I knew I shouldn't have come here. You clearly can't help me deal with Diablo."

"The devil?"

"If one more person says that... Yes, the devil. When I couldn't solve the equation to make time travel possible, he took me to an abyss where I could go back in time. I had to sign a contract to use it. I get only three times to use it. I used one to go back in time, another to come back to the present. I have one more, but he refuses to take me back to the abyss."

"Why does he refuse?"

"Because he loves the world as it is. Millions died without converting to Christ. If I go back and change, those millions will have a chance to convert."

Pastor Howard laughed, "Well, whatever fictional story you're writing sounds good."

"Fictional story? Look around you, Pastor Howard, people are dying and it's on me."

"Son, it's on you because you created the cure. Not because you traveled back in time." The office went silent. DJ realized it was senseless to argue with Pastor Howard. He was set in his thinking and could not grasp that the supernatural world existed within their world. He believed in God and trusted his faith, but when it was time to fight, he did not believe.

DJ stood, "Thank you for your time." He walked toward the door.

"Wait. Come back and let's talk some more."

DJ stopped and thought about it. He gave him another chance. "What good is it to talk when you don't believe what I'm telling you? I met the devil and I'm not proud of it. What I need is someone to help me return to the abyss."

"You say you signed a contract, right?"

"Yes."

"Where is it? If you want to prove to me you signed a contract with the devil, then produce it."

DJ reached into his back pocket. He kept the contract there in case he needed it. He handed the paper to Pastor Howard and Pastor Howard opened it and looked at it. "There's nothing on this paper."

"What?" DJ grabbed the paper from Pastor Howard. He looked at the paper with disbelief. "How can this be? I sighed it in red ink."

Pastor Howard sat up at his desk and folded his fingers. "Son, let me ask you a question. Let's say all this you say is real, right?"

"Yes, it is real."

"Then you signed that document before you jumped into the abyss and went back in time. Then you changed the events surrounding your father's death and returned to this time."

"Yes, that's how it happened."

"Then the paper is blank because you didn't sign it in this timeline."

DJ thought. Pastor Howard was right. In this timeline, he never pursued time travel, therefore he never met Diablo and signed a contract with him. But if he did not have a contract, how could he convince Diablo to give him another shot and the abyss? "You are right, Pastor Howard, but that doesn't help me. The world is in shambles, and Diablo is the only one who can take me to the abyss."

"Are you sure about that?"

"As sure as I can be."

"DJ, there's good and there's evil. The devil doesn't hold all the cards. God has them too. If he wants you to find the abyss then you will find it without Diablo's help. You just have to be open to God's word."

"What does that mean?"

"That means, it's time for you to give your life to him."

"I don't have a life to give him, remember? I signed that—"

"That contract doesn't exist now."

Could this be the loop hold DJ needed to get out of the contract? DJ smiled at Pastor Howard's words. He said, "Pastor, I don't know anything about Christ. My mother took me to church when I was a kid, but I was enamored with science and didn't believe any of it. I always believed that science was the answer to everything in this world."

Pastor Howard laughed, "No son, science can explain most of what God has created, but for the complete picture you need God." He reached into his desk and pulled out a Bible. He wrote inside it and handed it to DJ. "You like to read; I can see it in your spirit. Read this and come back and see me. Then we can save your soul."

DJ took the Bible in his hands and shivered. He did not understand what happened to him, but he felt a change inside from touching the Bible. He embraced it. "I will, Pastor Howard, and thank you for your time."

Pastor Howard nodded. DJ stood and walked out of the office. Gabriel stood just out the office door. He smiled at DJ. DJ asked, "Do we know each other?"

"Maybe in another life."

The answer made DJ question if Gabriel recognized him from their meeting. It could not be possible, but since he looked the same age he did when they met in the past, but anything was possible. DJ walked away but stopped and looked back. Gabriel and Pastor Howard talked. *"They know each other."*

Chapter 13

DJ sat inside his car and opened the Bible Pastor Howard gave him. The words simply read Romans 10:9-10. He flipped to the verse and read it, *"That if you confess with your mouth, "Jesus is Lord," and believe in your heart that God raised him from the dead, you will be saved. 10 For it is with your heart that you believe and are justified, and it is with your mouth that you confess and are saved."*

DJ embraced the words. He remembered them from the days he was forced to go to church. He looked up to the sky and asked, *"God, help me. I know I messed up your plan. I caused millions to die without salvation. That was never my intention. It is not true that some things are yours to attend to. Everything under the sun is yours to attend to and if you get me out of this, I will sacrifice my life and go back in time to fix this world."*

DJ hoped God heard his words. He did not know how to pray, but he believed if he talked to God like a person, He would hear his cry.

DJ pulled his car out onto the roadway and slammed on the brakes. Diablo stood in front of the car. His face was tight, and anger was evident. He walked around and got inside the vehicle. DJ refused to make eye contact. Diablo said, "You think you can get out of this contract? I own you and that pastor has no idea what power I have on this Earth."

"The contract is blank, therefore there is no proof I signed it. My soul is mine."

Diablo shouted, "Your soul is mine!"

Diablo's voice was loud and eerie. It brought chills to DJ's body. He was nervous. DJ never faced death before, but he surely believed he was going to die.

The car grew silent. DJ looked to the passenger side; Diablo was gone. DJ felt relieved. He sped off, headed back to Jeff's place.

When he arrived, he found Jeff slumped over his lab table. "Oh, Jeff man. Not another person I've lost. God guide me to the abyss."

Jeff jumped up. "Hey, was I sleep?"

"Dude, you scared the heck out of me again. I thought you were dead."

"No, I've been working all day and night."

"That doesn't look like science."

"It's not. I went to this Catholic church and found these books. They talk about the edge of the universe. Isn't that where you said Diablo told you the abyss was located?"

"Yeah, you gave up on science."

"Science can only take you so far. If you're serious about going back in time and dying there to make this right, then I have to help you. Too many people are dying out here."

"Actually, I don't think I will die. The contract I signed is blank now. That means I signed it in the other timeline, but in this timeline it doesn't exist. Something Diablo conveniently left out."

"Interesting. Then the deal is off. If we find this abyss, you can change things back to their original path, come back and live out your days."

"Exactly. The hard part is finding this abyss."

Jeff sighed, "You know Diablo will not make it easy for us to find it either."

"That… I already know."

DJ and Jeff searched the books for hours. Neither of them realized it was two in the morning. DJ looked at Jeff and he was fast asleep again. When DJ closed the book he was reading, he saw Diablo sitting across from him. "You seem to visit more. Does that mean I'm getting close?"

"I'm not concerned about you finding the abyss. Its location is unknown to any human. Only a supernatural being like myself can guide you there."

"Then why all the appearances? Oh, I know, you lost my soul and now you're concerned that I'm going to heed the words of Romans and be saved."

"I own your soul no matter what timeline you are in."

"So, you say, but you have nothing in writing to show that. Now, if you show me the abyss and allow me to go back in time, you can have that document again."

Diablo laughed, "I don't need your soul. I have millions I wouldn't have had if it were not for you."

"So be it." DJ stood. "There is no reason for you to be here any longer. Goodbye."

Diablo replied, "I go when I want."

DJ was full of himself. He had a renewed courage that did not exist before, "I remember my mother saying that the faith of a mustard seed is all that is required to move a mountain. In that case, I have the faith to tell you, 'Get out Satan!'"

DJ smiled as Diablo disappeared from his present. "This supernatural stuff works. You just need to believe. God, I know you're going to fix this for me."

Jeff said, "What are you doing, man?"

"You're awake."

"Yeah, you woke me up. Where do we stand?"

"I need to go see Donna."

"Dude, she may be in her last hours. Do you really want to see her like that?"

"I do. I want to tell her everything will be fixed."

"How, you have a clue?"

"No, but I know I will find the abyss and fix everything. She won't be with me, but she will be alive."

Jeff nodded his head, "You have a renewed confidence."

"I do. I'll chat with you later." DJ rolled out of the house and headed back downtown. This time the drive was without any people on the street. There were abandoned cars and bodies of the dead everywhere. *"I wonder how many people are still alive."*

DJ pulled his car in front of the lab building. There were no protesters now and no security guards. Those that were alive were with their families. DJ raced inside and headed up to the elevator. He found several bodies in the hallway and called out, "Donna. Donna, are you here?"

There was a woman sitting on the floor. She was barely alive. "Ma'am, can you hear me?"

"Yes."

"Do you know Donna James?"

"She left a while ago. Said she was going to look for her husband."

"I'm her husband."

"She left with a man… his name… I can't remember, but it was a strange name."

DJ was puzzled. Why would she leave with anyone? "What did the man look like?"

"He was dressed very well. I loved the black suit with the red tie. It looked good on his athletic body."

DJ felt a pit in his stomach. "Was his name Diablo?"

"That's it. It was a strange name. He promised her she would not die from the virus. I told her the man was crazy."

DJ whispered, "Oh, no."

"I'm sorry." The woman fell over. Her dying words were to tell DJ his wife in this timeline left with Diablo.

He raced to his car. DJ knew Diablo was doing this to get revenge on him. *"What does he want with Donna? She had nothing to do with this."* Once in his car, he had no idea where he was going. He ended up near the Lago de Fuego restaurant. *"Somehow I always end up here or the park."* He stopped the car and got out. The night was breezy, but DJ did not mind. He only wanted to get Donna back.

Minutes later, Diablo showed from nowhere with a grin on his face. He held Donna's arm as she staggered alongside of him. "So, you have come to my place to retrieve your wife."

"Leave her out of this."

"She is part of this. You have something I want, and now I have something you want."

"I'm not giving you, my soul."

"Then I shall have hers."

"You can't get hers unless she gives it to you and from the looks of it, she's not in any condition to do that."

Diablo reared his head back, "That may be true, but she's not saved either. If I kill her, she will be mine anyway." He pulled out a knife and held it to Donna's throat. "How about I slice her pretty little throat?"

"God won't allow you to do that. You need someone to do your work for you."

"So, you've been studying."

"I have, and I know God is real. He will save this world and somehow correct the mistake I made."

Diablo laughed loudly into the night. "You are sadly mistaken, my friend. The souls that have succumb to the James' Virus are mine. They died without salvation. They died without believing in Christ. I own them forever."

"Let her go."

"Give me a reason to let her go."

"What reason would that be?"

"Your soul. You know the price."

"Earlier you said you had millions, and my soul was of no consequence to you. Now you seem to want my soul badly."

"Again, you are mistaken. The more souls I get, the better. One million and one is better than one million, would you not agree?"

"I would, but something about this entire thing since I got here has not sat right with me. I have my suspicions."

"What are those suspicions?"

"I'd rather keep that information to myself for a while. One thing is for sure, you will not have my soul or Donna's. Let her go."

"I refuse."

DJ looked around and his suspicions about the world he was in continued to grow. "You know Diablo, I'm a scientist and I'm trained to observe. I have observed many things since I got here. So let me tell you this: I will find the abyss on my own. I don't believe you can hurt Donna, therefore…" He opened his car door and got inside, "She is safe with you." He started his car and prepared to drive off.

"I will slit her throat," yelled Diablo.

"No… you won't. You need a human to do it. You can't do it on your own and Donna is too strong to succumb to your will." He drove off, listening to Diablo yell into the night air.

DJ arrived back at Jeff's place. Jeff had contracted the virus. DJ said, "Jeff, how did you get the virus?"

"I don't know, man. I've been careful. This thing must be airborne. That's the only way."

"Have you left the house?"

"No, I've been here since you left."

More confirmation for DJ. He knew what was going on, but he did not know how to get out of it. "Jeff, I think I know how to get to the abyss."

"How?"

DJ moved to a chair near Jeff. He said, "All I have to do is close my eyes and think about the abyss. Before Diablo guided me there because I wanted to go there. I think I don't need him. I think I can will myself there on my own."

"How can you do that?"

"I can't explain now, but someday, I'll tell you all about it."

DJ leaned back in the chair and closed his eyes. He focused on nothing but the abyss. Diablo appeared in his mind and attempted to distract him. Diablo said, "This won't work. You don't have the ability to do this." DJ continued to focus on the abyss, using all the mental powers to tune out Diablo. Diablo continued, "You can't do it; you won't be successful, you will fail." He continued to pour negativity into DJ's spirit, but DJ's powers to focus would not allow it. He realized he was on to something because Diablo would only try to stop him if he could succeed. His faith was strong.

In a flash, DJ stood in front of the abyss. "I knew it. I knew I could get back here. If here really exists." DJ moved to the edge of the abyss.

Diablo said, "So you got here, but remember, you only have one jump left. There is nothing you can do about that. You won't see your pretty little Donna or Tameka again." DJ smiled at Diablo. "Why are you smiling?"

"Because I have figured all of this out. I'll make this jump and fix what I messed up. Then I will return to see that everything is right as it should be."

"If you jump into the abyss, you will never see your family again. In 48 hours, you will cease to exist. I will still have Donna's soul. I will win.

"I'm not a Bible scholar, but my mother dragged me to enough church services to learn that the devil is a liar. I believe you are lying right now." DJ turned and looked into the abyss. His window of time was approaching. "Here I go. See you back in time."

DJ jumped into the abyss. Like the two previous times, the ripples of time pulled him back and forth. There were times when he was not sure he would make it, but as always, he did. He fell to the ground near his old home. The people were alive and there were no signs of disease.

DJ stood. He looked around. No one seemed to notice he appeared out of thin air. He wondered what day it was. Was he in time to watch his father murdered? This time, he would not interfere.

Diablo appeared. "I love to watch this over and over. I swear your father dies better in this timeline than he did in that hospital bed. What is this the third time you get to watch him die?"

"Leave me alone."

"Why would I do that?"

"Yeah, why would you?"

"You can stop this, you know. For the price of your soul, I will allow you to stay longer than 48 hours. That way, you can stop your mother from going to the lab and contracting cancer. Your dad never gets obsessed with creating the cure, and the world remains a sickeningly happy place. Deal?"

"No deal. I'm not selling my soul."

"You mean again?"

"I'm not selling my soul to you ever again."

"Here comes my impressionable friend. Maybe this time I'll have him kill both of you. Now, how would that turn out?"

"Job."

"What?"

"You can only do what God allows you to do. It's in Job. If you didn't kill me the first time, it was because you were not allowed to do so."

"Interesting… someone paid more attention in church than they let on."

"I did, but I forgot most of it. I believed it was mumbo jumbo. After dealing with you, I know it's all true."

"That Bible isn't true. Men wrote that crap. You all are fools to read it."

"It hasn't let me down dealing with you. Since Pastor Howard put it in my hand, I've felt a renewed spirit. A spirit that I can do all things and you can't stop me."

"I'm about to throw up, but wait… here comes the good part."

The man approached Derek Sr. and the younger DJ. DJ did not want to watch his dad die for the third time, but he could not bring himself to stop. He believed it was his punishment for pursuing time travel. Now he had to suffer through his father's death a third time. Not to mention seeing Tameka die. It did not matter to him if he could exist for two days; he just knew this was the right thing to do. He had to allow God's work to be done.

The man fired the shot into Derek Sr. and DJ gasp as his father fell to the ground. He watched the man say something to the younger version of himself and get into the car. The man drove away. DJ wanted to go after him and kill him, but he could not. Even if he now knew the truth, he still wanted to go after the man.

Diablo said, "Well, you have righted your wrong. Now it's time to disappear into nothingness."

"I don't believe you. I will find somewhere to hang out. Somewhere you won't dare go." DJ walked away. He knew the place he wanted to spend his last hours. A place he believed Diablo would not come.

ACTIONS HAVE CONSEQUENCES

Chapter 14

DJ arrived at True Gospel church. It took him longer to get there since he did not have a car, but it did not matter to him. He had less than two days to exist and he would rather spend it at the church.

The building looked different in this time. It was newer. DJ walked inside. The only person present was sitting in the first row. He stood and approached DJ. "Welcome."

DJ replied, "Thank you. I just wanted somewhere to wait for the next couple of days. Do you mind if I sit here for a while?"

"No, son. You can wait as long as you like." DJ took a seat in the first row with the man. He asked, "So what's your name, son?"

"Derek... um, just call me DJ."

"Good, good... I'm Pastor Howard."

DJ was stunned. *"This can't be the same man."* DJ replied, "It's good to meet you, sir."

"It's good to meet you, too. You caught me at a good time. I was here praying for my wife. She's about to have my son."

"Really, that's awesome."

"Yeah, I'm going to name him after me. He'll be a junior and hopefully a man of the cloth."

DJ smiled, *"His son, which makes sense."* He said to Pastor Howard, "Yes, sir. I have this strange feeling he will be a powerful man of the cloth."

Pastor Howard asked, "So, what brings you here? I don't think I've seen you here before."

"I've never been here. I came by because I have some bad news. They said I won't live much longer, so I want to stay here, you know, close to God."

"Oh, my. I'm sorry to hear that, but God is everywhere, and He can heal anything."

"My mother used to say that all the time. My father was told by doctors that he couldn't have children, but ten months later my mom was pregnant with me. That says a lot about God and doctors."

"Yes, it does." Pastor Howard paused, "What do you have?"

"Oh, some long unpronounceable name, but does it really matter in the grand scheme of things?"

"I guess not." The door opened and Pastor Howard stood. "Grand Central today." He went to the door and out of DJ's view, but he could hear the pastor speaking.

Pastor Howard walked back inside, "Hey, DJ, we have another visitor today." DJ did not look up from the Bible he pulled out to read. "His name is Levi."

DJ looked up to shake the man's hand and froze in place. He looked at the man in disbelief.

Levi asked, "Haven't we met somewhere before?"

DJ answered, "You can't be here."

Levi replied, "Apparently you didn't read that Bible as well as you thought. I think you quoted me, Job earlier. You probably should reread that beginning." He turned to Pastor Howard, "So, Pastor Howard, how have you been? Still looking at little girls?"

"What? I don't do that."

"The correct response would be, 'I don't do that anymore.' You know God isn't the only one who sees all."

Pastor Howard asked, "Who are you?"

DJ said, "The devil. He introduced himself to me as Diablo. He's the reason I will cease to exist in a day and a half."

Pastor Howard fell to his knees and started praying. Diablo said, "I don't know how many people do that. They think it will get rid of me."

"How can you be in here? This is a church."

Diablo grinned, "If I can be in Heaven; why can't I be in here? You humans teach that the church is sacred ground, but it isn't. I come in here all the time and influence people to sin. Who do you think influenced good old Pastor Howard here to sin with that 15-year-old?" He laughed.

"God forgave him."

"Yeah, but his temptation will return and there will be another little girl to get him to sin. He's easy, but I'm having a hard time with you. I'm going to need to step up my game." He turned and walked out the church.

DJ wondered what he meant by stepping up his game. He would cease to exist in 30 hours, but he believed he could hold on.

DJ walked over to Pastor Howard. He was still at the altar praying. DJ's heart hurt for him. "Pastor, he's gone. You can get up now."

Pastor Howard stood. The look of embarrassment wore on his face. "I know I sinned with that young girl and I'm so sorry. I just let my lust overtake me. I'm not fit to be in the Kingdom."

"God has forgiven worse. You have to be strong. He's going to tempt you again. Whatever you need to do, do it. Don't let him have your soul."

Pastor Howard looked up at DJ, "You're a strong soldier for the Lord. I admire you, young man."

"Well, I have just recently begun to trust God. This is all new still but there's one more hurdle for me and I'm guessing after 30 hours I will find out if I am right about what I believe is happening to me."

"What do you believe is happening?"

"I'd like to keep that under wraps right now. Let's just sit here and talk."

Pastor Howard said, "That sounds fine with me. You know, I can honestly say that I have never knowingly been face-to-face with the devil. It's a heart wrenching thing to do."

"Yeah, I guess so, but since I didn't know he was the devil, it didn't bother me. Now, I know he lies every time he opens his mouth, so I'm sure he's lying about what will happen to me."

"You're sure about that?"

"I am. He told me he has millions of new souls because the virus killed them before they could repent. But why does he want my soul so bad? I can't answer that question. I believe when I do, all the answers will come to me."

Pastor Howard asked, "Virus, what virus?"

"Sorry, that's a long story for another time."

"Have you prayed?"

"I don't even know how to pray, Pastor Howard."

Pastor Howard stood, "Well, we have to fix that, son." Pastor Howard went to his office and retrieved a document. He said, "Okay, we have four steps that can help you learn how to pray. Talk to God, thank Him, ask him for what you need or want, then close your prayer in the name of Jesus. It's that simple, son. Keep this card on you at all times until you have it down."

"Thank you, Pastor Howard."

Pastor Howard's cell phone rang. He answered. DJ sat looking at the altar. He wondered what his timeline was like now. Was it all fixed? What was Tameka doing? He had so many questions that needed answers, but he needed to wait until his time was up.

Pastor Howard said, "My baby is here. I have to go to the hospital."

"That's wonderful Pastor. I can go somewhere else and wait. Thank you for allowing me to sit with you."

"You're welcome. I wish you all the best, son."

"Thank you, Pastor." DJ walked out of the church and headed down the street. His countdown was down to 24 hours. He sat in the park and watched the water on the lake. It was soothing to him. In minutes, DJ drifted off to sleep.

DJ saw himself at the bar again. The dream continued to haunt him. He drank and pondered about the state of his marriage with Tameka. He saw himself walking out of the bar and to his car. He rode down the street and as usual, a sudden stop woke him from his dream.

A cold sweat rolled down the side of DJ's face. He fought to regain his breath and struggled to resist passing out. *"I must be delirious. I'm hearing things. Tameka, Tameka… is that you?"*

He smiled, thinking he heard her voice again and again, calling his name. Then he heard his mom's voice, and a sense of comfort overcame him. Two women he loved were calling to him from the grave. He realized it must be Diablo playing with him again. He shot up and stood to his feet. DJ looked around, expecting to see his nemesis. In the distance, there was a man. He looked like Gabriel.

DJ headed toward Gabriel. Before he could reach him, Diablo stood before him. "It is time for you to die, my friend."

DJ looked at his watch. He slept for almost a day. "I'm ready for anything and I give my life to Jesus!"

Diablo shouted, "Noooo!"

Chapter 15

DJ stared at the light at the end of the tunnel. He wasn't sure if he should walk through it or not. He remembered near death stories of people seeing a light, but he could not remember if they walked into it or not. This light felt warm and inviting. There was a sense of comfort emitting from the light. A man tapped him on his shoulder. He looked at Him. Part of DJ's brain remembered the man but yet he knew he never saw Him before. Without the movement of His lips, He said, "It is not yet time."

As quick as He came, He left. DJ heard voices surrounding him. Some familiar, some not. He believed he was dreaming when he heard Tameka crying. She talked to him as if he were dead or dying. His 48 hours ran out, but why was he hearing people crying for him? *"What's happening to me? I'm not in the abyss, but I am supposed to have ceased to exist."*

DJ struggled to open his eyes. The room was blurry, and people were milling about their business. No one paid much attention to him. He glanced to his left and his eyes popped. He said, "Tameka?"

She turned and shouted, "DJ! You're awake!" She hugged him and kissed him on his face.

DJ was confused. He asked, "What's going on? When did I get back? I was supposed to cease to exist."

They all looked at each other. The nurse said, "Well, I don't know what you mean, Mr. James, but I need to take your vitals."

DJ pushed her hand away, "Donna? You're alive?"

Donna replied, "Um, I don't think we know each other, do we?"

"What?" DJ's head flopped back on the pillow. Donna took his vitals. "How long have I been in this bed?"

Donna said, "Three weeks since the accident."

DJ looked at her, then at Tameka. "Accident? What accident?"

Donna eased away. Tameka moved in, "Honey, we had a major blowout, and you left the house angry. You went to a bar and had a few drinks. From there, the bartender said you left. They found you in a ditch on the side of the road. Police said someone slammed into you and left the scene. You've been here in a coma since."

"So, I didn't time travel?"

Tameka nodded her head, "Honey, the talk of time travel caused our blowout. Let's not go there again."

"Trust me, I won't go there at all."

Tameka said, "Here's your doctor."

"Hi, DJ, I'm Dr. Gabriel. It's good to meet you."

DJ couldn't believe his eyes. This was Gabriel from his dream. He must have pulled people into his coma-like dream and inserted them into the storyline. He said to himself, *"But it seemed so real."*

Dr. Gabriel asked everyone in the room to leave out for a moment while he examined DJ. They all complied. When the room was empty, Dr. Gabriel said, "That's because, it was real. Everything you experience in that supernatural world was real. God gave you a revelation of what would happen if you proceeded with your mission to time travel. Some things are better left for God."

"You're an angel, aren't you?"

"I am."

"Why did Diablo… Satan want me so bad?"

"Because in the revelation you experience, none of the souls were actually his. He wanted the only soul he could have in your supernatural state, yours. You did well to resist."

"I noticed somethings weren't right. I believe my subconscious was telling me it wasn't real."

"That's just it; it was real, but it wasn't real. Hard for the human mind to accept, but if you had given your soul away, you would be obligated to honor it."

"But I signed the contract?"

"The contract was worthless because it was based on lies. Satan knew that and that's why he needed you to give your soul willingly, without the lies."

"Thank you, Dr. Gabriel."

"Gabriel is fine. You'll be released in a few minutes."

"Thank you. I've learned my lesson. All things should be left to God."

Author Bio

Gerald C. Anderson, Sr. was born and raised in Tampa, Florida. He spent most of his childhood life growing up in the Belmont Heights area of Tampa.

In 1980, Gerald graduated from C. Leon King Senior High School in Temple Terrace, Florida. Following graduation, he enlisted in the United States Air Force.

Air Force Life

In his service career, Gerald traveled the world with assignments to California (twice), Florida, Kansas, Maryland, West Germany, and Korea. Upon his last assignment in Maryland and after retirement from the Air Force, Gerald began working in the United States Federal Government's Department of Energy. In 2003, he moved to the Internal Revenue

Service, and in 2007 he joined the Department of Education.

Education

In 2005, Gerald got his Bachelor of Science degree in Computer Information Systems from Strayer University, and in 2008 he received his Master of Administration degree in Criminal Justice Administration from the University of Cincinnati (UC).

Published Books

We Come in Peace

27 Hours (What Would You Do If You Faced the End?)

Standing Firm (One Family's Fight Against Domestic Violence)

Secrets (Silent Screams in The Dark)

The Last Song

The Lawyer

Saved

The Room

Are You Innocent?

The Compendium Series

Weight Loss

Warlord

The Last Honorable Man

The Dream

The Death Knights

Twins

The Ride Along

Creative Inspirations

Fatal Misperceptions

Love & Lust

Where is Erica Cousins (Kindle Vella Story)

A Saved Man

In 1992, Gerald turned his life over to Jesus Christ and a life with Christ at the head. He is a church musician. He continues to live in Maryland with his son.

Thank You!

I would like to take this opportunity to thank you for reading my novella. "Actions Have Consequences" was written to entertain my Christian fanbase. I hope I accomplished this goal, and you have enjoyed the story and maybe learned something from it.

Please consider reading my previous novels and short stories listed at the front of this novel. I also manage a Christian lifestyle magazine, "The Lyfe Magazine" (www.thelyfemagazine.com).

Lastly, if you enjoyed this novella, please go to Amazon, and write me a review. Reviews help move novels, novellas, and short stories on Amazon so that other potential readers can find it.

Thank you so much and always have a blessed day!

Gerald C. Anderson, Sr.